Adventures With the Winglets

By
Carolyn Neuman

Order this book online at www.trafford.com
or email orders@trafford.com

Most Trafford titles are also available at major online book retailers.

Printed in the United States of America.

ISBN: 978-1-4669-6753-3 (sc)
ISBN: 978-1-4669-6754-0 (e)

Trafford rev. 11/08/2012

 www.trafford.com

North America & international
toll-free: 1 888 232 4444 (USA & Canada)
phone: 250 383 6864 ♦ fax: 812 355 4082

To Grandma Neuman—
for urging me to write about the old tree by
the snowball stand from which the magic came

<u>Part 1</u>

Passing Through Trees

Chapter 1

"I'm never speaking to you again!" Chrissy cried as she flung herself up the steps. She found her new bedroom and flopped on the bed.

Chrissy's parents had been talking about moving for weeks, but she never expected them to actually do it, especially right before winter break. Chrissy had been making up reasons with everything she could think of about why they shouldn't move. Russ and Alex, Chrissy's older brothers, had been doing the same, but they had finally caved in to the might of "The Parents."

So they had moved from Jackson, Mississippi to "Out-In-The-Middle-Of-Nowhere," Colorado. It was ruining her winter break. Just thinking about it again made her angry. Chrissy was still fuming as she began unpacking.

* * *

Over the next few days, the family brought in box after box after box filled with clothes, pictures, games, dishes, everything. On the fourth night, everyone lay on the grass in their huge backyard. Everyone, that is, except Chrissy, who was sitting in the hollow at the base of the only tree in the backyard. The old, twisted tree was the perfect size for her.

She was watching a worm wriggling through the pile of dirt that she had overturned on the ground. "Chrissy?" her mom called.

As Chrissy lifted her head to glance up at her mom, something in the grass caught her eye. It was a white rock, glinting in the light of the full moon. She picked it up and brushed the dirt off. It fit perfectly in her hand, and had a warm, tingly feeling. Suddenly, a cold breeze whistled through her hollow. Chrissy stood up, put the rock in her pocket, and marched to the back door.

*   *   *

The next morning, the cold wind continued, bringing with it a beautiful blanket of snow. Grumbling about needing a map to get to breakfast, Chrissy poured herself some Cheerios, plopped into a chair, and flicked on the small T.V. on the counter.

A loud THWAK! on the wall brought Chrissy to attention. She jumped up, ran to the window above the sink, and pushed back the pale green curtains. Russ and Alex had been shoveling snow from the driveway. They had been having a contest about who could throw their snow the highest, when Russ's shovelful hit the house. Then they had scrambled under the window where Chrissy wouldn't see them. When they jumped up and started yelling, Chrissy squealed and jumped, but her fright soon evaporated as fury took reign.

Chrissy scrambled to the hall closet, pulled on her coat, shoved her feet into pair of snow boots, and stomped outside. Neither Russ, nor Alex was out front; their shovels lay discarded on the side of the driveway. Chrissy stepped behind the house. That was her mistake.

The moment they saw her, Russ and Alex pummeled Chrissy with snowballs. She screamed and jumped back around the corner of the house. "Oh you are on!" she muttered to herself.

Chrissy made as many snowballs as she could hold, and then carefully stepped around the corner. She started throwing them, running and ducking her brothers' snowballs.

Suddenly, one of Chrissy's snowballs hit Alex smack in the chest. He fell to his knees, panting. Russ ran over to him. "He's not hurt, it's just a trick!" Chrissy called to Russ. "Right Alex?" she sounded unsure now.

Chrissy walked over to Alex and bent over him. "Chrissy?" Alex whispered. "If I go, would you do something for me?"

Chrissy looked wary of him. "What?" As he lay on his back, Alex fingered the snowball in his hand.

"Stay still."

As Chrissy was pondering this, Alex sat up and crushed the snowball over Chrissy's head. Jumping up, he darted around the house. Chrissy ran after Alex, yelling all the way, leaving Russ doubled over with laughter.

*   *   *

By the time their mom called them in for lunch, Chrissy had yelled herself hoarse, and they all were numb and panting. Before Chrissy's ears were even thawed, they were finished lunch, and Russ, Alex, and their dad were out shoveling the neighborhood sidewalks.

With no friends to play with, and her mom sewing by the fire, Chrissy ambled upstairs to her room. As she looked around for something to do, her eyes landed on the rock she had left on her bedside table the night before. Then she got an idea.

Chrissy hurried to the basement where her dad was starting a workbench. She found a piece of wire and a cord of long, thin, leather. She sat on the floor and wrapped the wire around the rock. Then she tied the ends of the wire around the middle of the leather, which she tied around her neck.

Excited, Chrissy ran to the bathroom and looked at herself in the mirror. She was tall, freckly, and had blazing red hair that curled right under her chin. The white rock matched perfectly, she decided.

*　　*　　*

Later that afternoon, Chrissy put her snow stuff back on and trudged outside with a book. She went behind the house (making sure that Russ and Alex weren't there) and sat in the hollow of her tree. Between the gnarled branches were piles of loose snow, and Chrissy was sure not to move around too much for fear of it all landing on her head.

She liked to run the edge of her rock along the crevices in the bark, pretending that it was the key to a door in the tree. Her thoughts played along with the book she was reading, "*Harry Potter and the Goblet of Fire.*"

Without noticing it, Chrissy found a notch in the tree where the rock fit in perfectly. She pushed it in. Suddenly the ground beneath her gave way and she crashed against the trunk of the tree. Chrissy caught her breath for a second, before the snow cascaded onto her head from the branches above.

Chrissy jumped up, brushing off the snow from her hair and face. As she bent down to pick up her book, she noticed a hole in the base of the tree. She wanted to inspect it, but right then her mom called her in for dinner. Grudgingly, she trudged back into the house.

The next morning, the sun was out, melting the snow into puddles. Chrissy spent most of the morning reading, watching T.V., and helping her parents. That wasn't exactly how she had wanted the morning to go, but after all, what can you do with half a snowfall and everything wet?

*   *   *

That afternoon, however, became warm and much drier, so Chrissy trooped outside with her book to the old tree. When she arrived, Chrissy remembered the new hole that appeared yesterday. She got onto her hands and knees to inspect it.

Chrissy tried to feel inside the hole, but whenever she seemed to have found an edge, it pushed farther back, melting to her touch.

When Chrissy finally sat back on her heels to look at it, she gasped; the hole was at least twice the width it had been when she first saw it. Well, great adventures start with great findings, don't they? Amazing discoveries start with curiosity, right? Chrissy started working again, this time really pushing the bark to make it wider and deeper.

Suddenly, with a mighty shove, a thin crack of light appeared all the way up the trunk of the tree. At first it was hard to see, but as Chrissy kept working, the silvery glow became thicker and thicker.

Chrissy then stood and put her entire weight on the crack. That did it! It was as if a door was specifically cut into the tree. The door swung open, and Chrissy tumbled inside!

Chapter 2

Chrissy scrambled to her feet. The door swung shut behind her without notice; in front of her, someone was standing, as confused as she was.

Chrissy could tell that it was a girl; she had flowing red hair down her back filled with beautiful beads. She had pointed, triangular blue eyes that were wide open and her mouth was agape in a giant "O." The girl had a necklace with a little spiral shell on it, and her clothes were mainly made of furs.

Chrissy found her voice first. "Hello," she said meekly.

The girl erupted. "Oh you're here, you're here, you're HERE! Oh Lisa, I've heard so much about you, but I *never* thought I would get to see you!" It seemed to take a great effort for her to pull herself together. "I'm Claudia. And you, of course, are Lisa!" she cried, holding out her hand.

"Lisa?" Chrissy thought to herself. "I wonder who she is . . ." Chrissy shook Claudia's hand, who in turn looked like she was going to faint.

Finally releasing Chrissy's hand, Claudia gestured behind herself. "Welcome to the Village of the Winglets!" She took the shell of her necklace to her lips and blew. Chrissy expected it to be a piercing high note, but instead it was a wonderful melody.

Immediately, movement behind Claudia captured Chrissy's attention. She gasped; the Village of the Winglets was made of a circle of twelve little cabins, with one magnificent tree-house in the center. Dense woods surrounded the circle of cabins. The Winglet People were emerging from their cabins everywhere and rushing over to them. Chrissy was enveloped in hugs and cries of delight.

Finally, Chrissy was ushered into one of the cabins, and the rest of the village followed them in. Everything was made of marvelous woodwork, with beautifully intricate designs of vines and flowers. She sat down at the dining room table, and a mug of hot chocolate was pushed into her hands. Chrissy took one small sip. Oh, how wonderful that was! It tasted of chocolate, vanilla, and candy, and must have been the best flavor that had ever touched Chrissy's taste buds.

The owners of the cabin, a rosy woman by the name of Alivia and a stout man named Antony, sat down with Chrissy at the table along with Claudia. The rest of the village crowded around the table in the now cramped dining room.

Antony started his tale in a deep, mystic voice that silenced the room. "A long, long time ago, the ancient storytellers proclaimed the coming of an enchantress." His once blue eyes glinted gold. "This enchantress, they said, will come of another world, another time. She will lead us through our greatest triumphs, and our worst defeats. She will-"

Somewhere outside the cabin, they heard a whistle. It didn't sound like the quick, high notes of Claudia's whistle, but slow, deep, and mellow. Suddenly, in burst an old man.

His eyes roved over the scene of the entire village cramped in one dining room. Then his eyes landed on Chrissy. "Lisa!" he gasped. With his eyes alight, the man cried, "The Enchantress has finally come and you keep her cramped in this house!?! Let us have a banquet!"

Everyone cheered and started pushing to get outside. "That's Matthew," Claudia whispered in Chrissy's ear. "He's The Leader." They all trooped up into the huge tree-house.

Inside was a long table. There were many chairs around it, one for each of the Winglets with their name inscribed on the back. The table was already set, with dazzling silver plates, forks, and knives. What astounded Chrissy most was the pure gold goblet that stood at each place.

Once everyone was seated and silenced, Matthew performed a special ceremony, mumbling in a different language and using certain hand gestures. Chrissy took that time to look at the other Winglets. They all had triangular eyes and long hair. All the women and girls had beads woven into theirs.

Soon the feast began. There were so many exotic dishes passed along the table. It was all most delicious. Chrissy ate ravenously, devouring each new dish.

She really didn't understand this whole "lead us through our greatest triumphs and our worst defeats" thing, but they were talking about some Lisa girl who had nothing to do with Chrissy, and her family was going to be really worried if she wasn't back for dinner. Of course, they knew that she reads for really long periods of time, but not *that* long. And it would be too dark to read anyway.

Soon, people started rising with their plates. Chrissy followed them into a small room on the side of the tree-house that she hadn't noticed before. Inside, there was a shelf with a few extra plates on it, and a tub filled with a thick, bubbling, bright purple liquid.

Chrissy watched in amazement as each person in line dipped their plate into the tub. The liquid frothed wildly for a second, and then the plate was pulled out as clean as it was before the feast.

When Chrissy dunked her plate in, a little drop of the liquid splashed onto her hand. It was warm and tingly. Her plate dried instantly when she took it out, and Chrissy put it on the shelf with the others.

Chrissy headed outside. She started toward her tree, but Claudia stopped her. "Aren't you staying in my cabin? It's over there."

"Um, no Claudia. I'm really sorry, but I can't stay here." Chrissy started walking to her tree again.

Chrissy turned around when she got there, but soon wished she hadn't. Many surprised and disappointed faces looked back at her.

"Look, I'm not Lisa. My name is Chrissy, and I don't belong here. I don't know how I got here, but it was a mistake. Your food was great, and you've been really nice to me, but I have to go home. Sorry."

Chrissy turned to the great tree and leaned against it. The door opened, as she had expected it to. Chrissy quietly slipped through the doorway, back into her own world.

Chapter 3

$\mathcal{E}$verything was the same as when she left, except for the fiery sun sliding below the horizon. Chrissy's book still lay in the grass. She picked it up and slowly walked to her house. Her parents worried over her, but Chrissy simply said, "I accidentally fell asleep, but I'm not hungry."

*   *   *

The next day, Chrissy asked her Dad if she could go to the library. "Sure honey!" he replied. "It's just two blocks down the road. Would you like me to go with you?"

"No thanks," Chrissy replied. "I think I'll walk alone today." She pulled on her shoes and coat and stepped out into the cool morning air. Walking down the sidewalk gave her time to replay in her mind what had happened yesterday.

As she was browsing around the library, Chrissy noticed a girl sitting on the window ledge, reading. She had curly black hair and green eyes. She glanced up from her book, and their eyes locked.

"You can read it with me if you'd like. It's a good book," she said, lifting it so Chrissy could see the title, "Looking Back." Chrissy thought that sounded really boring, but she sat down next to the girl anyway. "Oh, and by the way, my name is Lisa," the girl said happily, sliding the book over so that they could both read.

Chrissy hesitated. That's weird, she thought, but it's just a coincedence. It has to be. There's no *possible* way that Lisa could have found a door in her tree too. After a slight pause, she said, "I'm Chrissy."

Leaning forward to read, Chrissy's rock necklace swung out from under her shirt. "That's a nice necklace," Lisa commented.

"Thanks." Even as Lisa read aloud for the both of them, Chrissy's thoughts strayed again to the Winglets. After all, she *had* been a little rude, and they had shown her great hospitality. She decided to go back and apologize. "Sorry, Lisa, but I have to go home. It was nice meeting you, and I hope we'll see each other again sometime."

Lisa's eyes sparkled. "Yes, I think we will see each other again. Bye!"

When Chrissy arrived in the backyard, Russ was collecting firewood. She pretended to mess around randomly until he left. Chrissy waited a little bit to be sure that he was gone, then turned to the tree. She pushed and heaved on it, but no door opened. She pushed so hard, Chrissy worried that the tree might fall over. She tried to remember everything she had done before. *The rock.*

Chrissy rushed inside and pounded up the stairs. She grabbed the necklace from her bedside-table and ran back outside. With fumbling fingers, Chrissy fit the rock into its hole. The silvery outline of a door suddenly burned on the tree. She pushed it open, and stepped through once again.

Chapter 4

livia saw Chrissy first. She was just coming down from the tree-house. She blew her whistle and ran over. Joyful shouts came from all over as everyone raced from the tree-house to see what was going on. Chrissy was engulfed in hugs from all sides. "I'm sorry-" she began, but nobody listened; they welcomed her in spite of the events of yesterday.

In the midst of everything, Chrissy felt a tug on her sleeve. It was Claudia. "Let's go inside," she whispered. They slipped out of the crowd and disapeared into Claudia's cabin.

In the living room, Chrissy sat on a beautiful wood sofa with velvet cushions. Claudia sat next to her. Staring at beautifully carved fish and dophins swimming about the table in front of them, an idea sprung into Chrissy's mind. "Hey Claudia," she asked, running her finger along the table legs. "Do you think you could teach me how to carve like this?"

Claudia looked thrilled. She jumped up and beckoned Chrissy to follow. They went into the kitchen. Claudia walked over to a locked drawer, quickly snapped the combination, and opened it. Inside were some knives, a knife sharpener, lots of wood shavings, and a half-whittled owl. Claudia took two knives and the owl.

When they sat back down on the couch, Claudia handed Chrissy one of the knives. "Did you make that owl?" Chrissy asked. Claudia blushed.

"It's not near as good as the things my mom makes."

"No, it's great!" Chrissy insisted.

Pulling herself together, Claudia said, "Anyway, when you choose your stick, you want it to be a little bit thicker than this." She pointed to her owl. "Go outside and see if you can find one." Chrissy stepped outside, and screamed. Her scream was quickly muffled as a hand clamped over her mouth.

Startled, Claudia jumped up and ran outside. The tree-house was on fire, and Chrissy was nowhere in sight!

Chapter 5

Claudia sounded her whistle, along with many other people around the village. Shouts echoed across the circle. "Fire! Fire!"

"Someone help!"

"Get more water!"

Claudia noticed Matthew running into his cabin. She was just about to follow him when she was pushed aside by her parents, who were rushing to help.

But oddly, Claudia noticed that with each bucket of water, the flames were getting higher and higher. "Stop!" she screamed.

*   *   *

She was sitting on cold, hard ground, tied to a tree. Chrissy could hear echoing shouts in the distance. She could barely see, but the dim outlines of trees were all around her. She was in a forest.

Chrissy had just reached this conclusion when a dry, rasping voice came out of the shadows. "She's come 'round."

"Oh has she?" asked another voice, colder and harder than the first. A man stepped in front of Chrissy.

He was tall and thin. Tiger skins were draped over his broad shoulders, and he had many gold rings on his long, white, bony hands.

Chrissy winced as the man ran his fingers through her hair. "Where is it?" he whispered in her ear.

"Where is what?" Chrissy's voice was surprisingly steady, but with anger coursing through it like fire. How dare this man kidnap her in a world she didn't even belong in!

"What else, but the key of course," the man growled.

"She has it with her," the first voice said quietly.

"What's that, Blockhead?"

"Wears it 'round her neck, she does, Luther," he said, louder this time.

The man called Luther delicately plucked the leather of Chrissy's necklace and pulled the rock out from under her shirt. "So she does," he breathed.

Luther lifted the necklace over her head and slipped it into his pocket. He left without a word, and Blockhead followed behind. Chrissy was left tied to the tree.

*   *   *

The fire was finally extinguished. Matthew was lost in thought, staring at the tree-house. Claudia heard him muttering, "Luther . . . not again . . . the old ways . . . but not now, can't be . . . there's nothing in there this time . . ."

Suddenly, Alivia shouted, "Where's Chrissy?"

Claudia started. She staggered forward. "I was . . . we were . . . she went outside," she blurted out. "And then I heard her scream, and I went outside to see what was wrong, and she was gone, and the tree-house was on fire, and—Oh Matthew, what do you think happened to Chrissy?"

A wave of whispers burst out around the circle. Claudia hung her head. Her parents came forward and led her inside.

*   *   *

She was staring at a chipmunk. She really was. And it was staring back. Seriously, it was just sitting there, right in front of her, eyes popping. Chrissy found herself asking the chipmunk, "So, are you just going to sit there staring at me, tied to a tree?"

The chipmunk jumped, and to Chrissy's enormous surprise, ran up the tree to where the ropes were tightly tied and began biting them vigorously. In seconds, the ropes fell to the ground.

Chrissy stood up, brushed herself off, and stretched. The chipmunk was on the ground again. His nose was scrunched up as if saying, "Those ropes tasted disgusting!" He then scampered away between the trees.

"Thanks," Chrissy whispered after him.

*   *   *

Her parents had gone back outside to see what was going on. Claudia was on the sofa with a cup of hot chocolate. Suddenly, Claudia heard a definite upswing in the noise outside, so she got up to see what was happening.

*   *   *

They were all crowded around her. Chrissy could see Claudia running over from her cabin. She was relieved to see all these welcoming faces, but her mind was mostly on where Luther was, and what he was doing. Suddenly, Chrissy saw him. With an angry shout, she started pushing through the crowd, but it was too late. The door to her world was already closing behind those horrible tiger skins!

Chapter 6

Chrissy kept her eyes closed. She was confused . . . and aching all over. The last thing she remembered was Luther disappearing through the tree, then feeling horribly sick.

She braced herself and opened her eyes. Chrissy was on the living room sofa, and her mom was fidgeting worriedly in a chair next to her. Relief spread over her face when she saw that Chrissy was awake. "Oh, honey-" she started to say, but Chrissy interrupted her.

"What happened?" she demanded.

"You never showed up for lunch, so I decided to look for you. I found you out by that old tree in the backyard. I carried you inside and you've been out for almost two hours!"

Chrissy suddenly noticed how hungry she was. "I'm starving!" she cried. Chrissy tried to sit up, but immediately flopped back down on the pillows.

"Now you stay right there, and I'll bring you your lunch," her mother told her firmly.

By dinner, Chrissy felt well enough to sit at the table to eat. Halfway through, she noticed a business card lying on the table. She picked it up and read:

```
┌─────────────────────────────────┐
│                                 │
│        Luther Rehtul            │
│        Tree Service             │
│       1-800-147-7326            │
│                                 │
└─────────────────────────────────┘
```

Immediately, she noticed two things. First, the name was Luther, and second, R-E-H-T-U-L was Luther spelled backwards.

Chrissy's dad noticed her looking at the card. "He came by earlier while you were out of it. Said that our old tree in the backyard was dangerous and had to come down. Odd man, really. He had an interesting outfit, especially for the middle of winter."

"What did he look like?" Chrissy whispered.

Her dad frowned. "Tall, thin. Wore a lot of rings. And I think it was tiger skins he was wearing." He shook his head. "Anyway, he took down the tree and hauled it away. Great service too, didn't cost us a dime!"

Chrissy sat there, devastated. "He also said that he found this in the grass," her mom added. "And I thought you might like it." She held up Chrissy's rock necklace.

"My ne—I mean, thanks Mom, I love it!" Chrissy cried, taking the necklace from her mom.

All night, Chrissy could hardly sleep. When she finally did, images of Luther's leering face and him chopping down her tree with relish swam across her mind. Chrissy woke up sweating.

Her mother had insisted that she stay in bed for a few more hours, so Chrissy reluctantly waited in her room while her mom made her breakfast. She was finally allowed to go at about eleven, and Chrissy raced outside, key in hand.

At last, Chrissy reached her tree. She couldn't believe it; all that was left of the doorway to her beloved Winglets was a gnarled old stump.

Chapter 7

Chrissy fell to her knees beside the stump and tried fiercely to fight back tears. A voice behind her said, "Aww, c'mon. It can't be that bad." Chrissy jumped. She turned around to tell Alex to go away when . . . it was Lisa.

"H-how-how did you . . ." Chrissy stuttered. Lisa smiled, but said nothing.

"And what do you mean, 'It can't be that bad'? This is horrible! How'm I supposed to get back?"

Lisa was about to speak when Chrissy's mom came out the back door and called, "Chrissy, stay away from that tree!"

Chrissy turned back to Lisa, but she had vanished. Chrissy stomped inside. "Why can't I be out there? It's just an old tree-stump!" Her mom didn't say anything.

*   *   *

After fuming in her room for a while, Chrissy got a wonderful idea. She went out to the front yard and found her perfect stick. In the kitchen, she took a sharp knife from the silverware drawer and ran back upstairs to her room.

Sitting on her bed, Chrissy closed her eyes. She found the perfect thing and pictured it in her mind. She saw every shape, curve, and line.

Eyes still closed, Chrissy let the knife flow like water over the wood. She never knew how she did it, but she never opened her eyes, and she never got cut. Wood shavings covered her lap, but Chrissy ignored them. When she finished, Chrissy put the knife down and ran a finger over her creation. Finally she opened her eyes.

Chrissy gasped. It was beautiful. It was perfect. A horse lay in her hands, mid-stride, mane streaming out behind it. Chrissy named her horse Alexis.

Chrissy dumped her wood shavings in the wastepaper basket and went downstairs. She put the knife in the sink just as her mom came in and said, "I'm going to the store. I'll be back in a little while."

"Okay." Now was her chance! Chrissy grabbed her rock key and Alexis and raced outside to the old tree-stump. She set Alexis down and paced around the stump, pondering how to get through.

"I'm back."

Chrissy jumped, expecting to see her mom, but instead, Lisa had just popped out of nowhere. "How do you do that?" Chrissy demanded, but again Lisa said nothing. Her silence was infuriating. "Are you going to tell me how to get back, or are you just practicing teleportation?"

Lisa smiled. "It's quite simple, really. You already have the key, so just make a lock!"

"And just how am I going to do that? Call a locksmith and tell him to put a lock on a tree-stump?"

Lisa laughed. "No really, think about it. Remember what you just did with Alexis?"

Chrissy didn't ask how she knew about Alexis, she just ran inside and got a knife, and came back out to the tree-stump. Closing her eyes again, Chrissy picked up the rock. She felt it in her palm. Placing the tip of the knife on the center of the stump, she started cutting.

Soon, there was a hole in the stump. It looked likely that the rock would fit. Chrissy put the rock above the hole, and Lisa watched in amazement as she set the rock perfectly in place.

Nothing happened. No silvery light. No openings into a different world. Nothing. Chrissy was stumped (no pun intended). She tried to remember everything that had happened before. Then she realized, the light was usually around the doorframe, but this time there wasn't any door. So maybe, if she made a door, it just might work.

Chrissy set the knife tip about an inch away from the edge of the stump. As soon as she pierced the surface, the silver light burst through the crack. Chrissy continued to carve the circle and the light filled every crevice. She finished the circle, and the light shone even brighter.

As she dropped the knife in the grass, Chrissy looked behind her, but Lisa was gone. Chrissy didn't stop to think and just picked up Alexis.

Soon, the stump was almost too bright to look at. Chrissy tried to take her rock out, but it seemed to be stuck in the hole. So instead, she took the leather loop and pulled, opening the tree like a trapdoor.

If she had looked back one more time, Chrissy would have seen her mother marching across the lawn. But she didn't. She jumped in without a backward glance.

Chapter 8

*T*here was no one in sight. Chrissy ran over to Claudia's cabin and knocked on the door. "Hello? It's me, Chrissy! Where is everyone?"

Instantly, the door opened and Claudia appeared. "SHHHHH!" She pulled Chrissy inside and closed the door quickly behind her.

"What's the matter?" Chrissy whispered. "What happened?"

"They're just having a meeting in the tree-house," Claudia said normally. Then she noticed something in Chrissy's hand. "What's that?"

Chrissy's ears turned pink, but she held it up for Claudia to see. "Her name is Alexis."

Claudia's mouth formed a silent "wow." Then her eyes lit up and she pulled Chrissy into the next room.

Inside, the room was dimly lit. There was a single table in the center of the room. On the table, a large basin was filled with the same purple liquid as the Winglets used to wash dishes in the tree-house.

They silently approached the table. Claudia whispered instructions, and Chrissy proceeded to drop Alexis into the basin, and she sank all the way to the bottom. The liquid fizzed and frothed and bubbled, then settled, turning clear.

But, instead of seeing Alexis at the bottom, they saw an image of a fierce, pure white mare prancing through fields with her foals.

Suddenly, the water began to churn. The image disappeared, and the liquid slowly turned back to purple. By now, it was a mini-whirlpool, and it began to drain. Alexis emerged at the bottom, still a wood horse. Claudia took Alexis from the now empty basin and raced outside. Chrissy followed her out.

Standing in the sunlight, Chrissy just noticed the tree-house, pristine and gleaming, perfectly rebuilt from the fire.

Claudia put Alexis on the ground. "Call her!" she said excitedly.

Chrissy was confused, but she called, "Alexis." Then she watched in amazement as the little wood horse she herself had carved transformed into the beautiful, fierce white mare they had seen in the basin, pawing and tossing her head and mane proudly.

Claudia pushed Chrissy forward, and she anxiously pulled herself onto Alexis's back. Alexis whinnied and started cantering around. Chrissy had always wanted a horse . . .

Soon, the meeting ended and Winglets streamed out of the tree-house. Chrissy and Alexis trotted over, but the Winglets did not rejoice like before. They just turned and looked at Matthew, who said, "Miss Chrissy, could I please have a private word with you? And I think it would be necessary to have Miss Claudia come too. We have some things to discuss."

Chrissy slipped off Alexis's back, and she and Claudia followed Matthew into his cabin. They proceeded through to the dining room and sat down. "After the events of your last visit, many questions have arisen. You are most likely wondering, 'What happened after Luther escaped?' You fainted. My guess is that after he left with your key and went into your world, it drained you of your energy. Antony had to carry you back through the door, but he was very nearly seen by your mother!"

"Luther cut down the tree," Chrissy blurted out. "And for some reason he gave me the key back."

Matthew smiled. "I believe Luther thought he made it impossible for you to get back, so he left you a reminder that he won. Obviously he must have misjudged your carving skills!"

"What's he going to do now?" Claudia asked.

"I know not, but you must be careful Chrissy. He is *not* a very nice guy."

Chrissy laughed. "Right. So who is this Lisa?"

"A very powerful enchantress. When she comes, she will help us all, and her magic will hopefully help us go back to the old ways."

Claudia's eyes were wide. "The old ways? Really?"

"Why? What're 'the old ways'?" Chrissy asked.

"Back when we used to practice magic and stuff. My parents told me about it. That was before . . ." Claudia trailed off.

"Before what? What happened?"

"Before Luther destroyed our practices," Matthew growled. "He burned the tree-house where we stored all our spell books and potions. It was the same fire that consumed our tree-house again yesterday . . ." He seemed to be lost in thought. Then he abruptly said, "You may go now."

Chrissy and Claudia stepped into the sunlight, and Alexis trotted over. As she stroked Alexis's mane, Chrissy said, "Y'know, I'm kinda glad that I moved. At first I really hated even the thought of it. But otherwise, I wouldn't have met all of you. You're my first friends since we came here."

Claudia agreed, "Yeah, I'm glad too. Even though you weren't who I thought you were at first, you're a great friend. Plus, you're a great carver!"

"Thanks. Actually I notice lots of people have 'at first' moments, but they really turn out all right!" Claudia smiled, and when Chrissy called Alexis, she shrank back into a wood horse, and Chrissy picked her up. They said good-bye to each other, and Chrissy faced the tree. Promising to return, Chrissy passed through the tree to her world once again.

To Aunt Fran-

for encouraging me to publish my work

Part 2

Dreams Tell the Future

Chapter 9

"The new girl" was sitting in the shade of the big maple tree next to the school blacktop. She had started school right after winter break, smack in the middle of the school year. Her family had moved here from Jackson, Mississippi, over a thousand miles from Colorado! What was her name again? Oh yeah, Chrissy.

*   *   *

Chrissy looked down at the things in her lap:
- A sharp knife
- Two thick sticks she had found around the tree
- Alexis, the little wood horse she had carved over winter break, frozen in mid-stride with her mane streaming out behind her

Chrissy planned to make two foals for Alexis, named Thunder and Lightning. She closed her eyes and pictured Thunder, a spirited black foal packed with energy like . . . well, thunder.

Chrissy picked up her knife and started carving. She worked in silence for minutes, shaving off pieces to form every detail of the foal. Wood chips covered her lap. Ending the tail with a flourish, Chrissy opened her eyes. Thunder lay in her hands, prancing happily. Chrissy stood him next to Alexis.

A shadow passed in front of her face. Chrissy looked up to see a girl with long, curly brown hair, and a stern look on her face. Immediately, the girl began scolding Chrissy. "Oh, you are in BIG trouble! I don't know what they do in Mississippi, but here, knives are SO not allowed."

"No, wait! I was-" Chrissy stammered, but then the girl's eyes landed on Alexis and Thunder.

"Oooooh!" she cried. "Did you make those?"

Chrissy blushed. "Yes, I carved them."

The girl picked up Alexis and felt her mane. "They're so life-like," she whispered. "What're their names?"

"That's Alexis, and this is Thunder."

"Wow." Then abruptly she said, "I'm Amanda, and I promise I won't tell anyone about the knife."

"Thanks," Chrissy said as she picked Thunder up and took Alexis from Amanda. "I'm Chrissy." Just then, they were called in from recess.

As Chrissy stood up and brushed the wood shavings off her lap, Amanda asked, "D'you want to do something together after school?"

"Um, sorry, but I'm . . . grounded."

"Oh."

"Yeah."

"Well, see you Monday then!" Amanda called, and they headed inside. Chrissy started to go in the door, but movement by the dumpsters caught her eye. She glanced over and saw a man with a pale, leering face. He was wearing tiger skins, and had rings on nearly every finger. Chrissy blinked, and he was gone.

*   *   *

Chrissy got off the bus and went straight to her room. After she dumped her backpack on her bed, Chrissy looked out the window at the old, gnarled stump of what *had been* the only tree in the backyard. Many events had passed through that tree. The image of the man by the dumpsters still burned in her mind, and she absentmindedly touched her rock necklace.

Chrissy thought back to the time over winter break when the stump was still a tree, and how she had discovered that the rock on her necklace was the key to the tree-door to another world. The Winglets welcomed her graciously there. Claudia had been teaching her how to carve wood when Chrissy was kidnapped by Luther, the very man she had seen at school today by the dumpsters! After Luther cut down the tree, Chrissy's mysterious friend Lisa helped her return to the Winglets through the stump.

Last time Chrissy came back to this world, she faced her mom in a towering rage. "I *told* you not to go near that tree!" her mom had stormed. "But you deliberately disobeyed me! I know you're upset about moving, but this is *not* the way to deal with it!" In the end, Chrissy had been grounded, and she didn't even know how long it would last.

She sighed and turned away from the window to start homework, but was startled to see a girl. She was standing with her back turned to Chrissy, fidgeting with something. Chrissy cleared her throat loudly, and the girl whirled around, startled. She had short, curly black hair and green eyes. She wore jeans, a plain purple t-shirt, and a weary but triumphant smile. Chrissy recognized her at once and hugged her old friend. "Lisa!" she cried. "It's been almost a month! What's up?"

Lisa's smile faded as she motioned them to sit down. "I have to tell you something. You see . . . well . . . Luther is my brother." Chrissy's jaw dropped to the floor, but Lisa held up a hand for her not to interrupt. "My mother and father were an enchantress and a sorcerer. When we were born, my parents gave Luther and me each a gift. Mine was a necklace, and Luther's was a ring. When I was eight, something happened and our parents turned to evil ways. They sent us away in fear that we might together become more powerful than they were."

"Tough parents," Chrissy muttered.

"I found a home with the Winglets, and taught them magic and sorcery. I was the one who began 'the old ways'.

"Luther, though, hid in the forest of Minakia, where he befriended the man he calls . . . Blockhead. Blockhead is a Quope, and Quopes are notoriously evil people. Luther lived with the Quopes for years as one of them, making himself an outcast amongst others."

Chrissy waited patiently for Lisa to continue.

"But you see, these gifts our parents gave us, they were linked. Luther found me with the Winglets, but Quopes were not welcome with the Winglets, and they wouldn't let him stay. Jealousy consumed him, and he became very angry. He sent many plagues upon the Winglets. I tried to help them, to stop Luther, but he was relentless."

"But how come you didn't get hurt?" Chrissy blurted out.

"My necklace protected me. The holder of one gift cannot directly harm the holder of the other gift. But I couldn't just let the Winglets suffer.

"As you know, Luther set fire to the tree-house, burning all our spell books and potions. That was when I left. I escaped into your world, using that tree." She pointed out the window. "The change in worlds confused Luther for a long time. Eight of your years, in fact."

"*My* years?"

"You only age in the world in which you were born. I have been fourteen for a long time.

"Anyway, eight of your years I've been here, and eight of your years Luther has been searching for me. He always kept a lookout on the Winglets' village. Then you came, and Blockhead saw you. He alerted Luther at once, and . . . you know the story from there. Now Luther is in this world, and he'll find me.

"But Chrissy, the reason I came; Luther is looking for my necklace. If he gets his hands on it, then combined with his ring, he'll have power—too much power! I've hidden it, and I'm going to go after him. I'll send someone to check in with you by tomorrow night. For now, goodbye." And she was gone.

Chrissy just sat there, stunned. She jumped as the door opened. Her mother stood in the doorway. "I thought I heard you talking to someone."

"No," Chrissy replied. "I was just . . . practicing for the spelling test."

"Oh." Her mom seemed uninterested. She sat down on the bed next to Chrissy. "You do know why you're grounded, right?"

"Sure, you didn't want me near a stupid old tree-stump."

"Yes, but that's not all. You didn't do what I told you. I don't know what happened last month, but it wouldn't have happened if you had stayed away from the stump like I told you in the first place. You have to learn to follow the rules."

"But why?" Chrissy cried. "What's wrong with that tree? Why can't I go near it?"

Her mom sighed. "There's something . . . strange about it, something . . . different. It's hard to explain, but I just don't like it."

They sat in silence for a while. Then her mom stood up and left abruptly. Chrissy sighed again and glumly started her homework.

Chrissy soon found out that homework wouldn't complete itself when you're not thinking about it, and math problems were definitely *not* on her mind. She *couldn't* tell her mom about the Winglets. The difference her mom was feeling around the tree was magic, and she couldn't tell that the magic was good. Chrissy knew, though. That magic was the best thing that had happened to Chrissy in her life. By six o'clock, Chrissy made up her mind to visit the Winglets again. Shoving her backpack aside, she grabbed Alexis and Thunder and sprinted down the steps.

At the bottom of the stairs, Chrissy glanced around to check that her mother wasn't around, then tip-toed toward the back door. In the hallway, Chrissy ran into her dad. "Oh, hi Dad." she said, trying to sound casual.

"Hello honey . . . shouldn't you be in your room?"

"Oh, well, I . . . bathroom." She hurried toward it, and her dad passed by. Chrissy breathed a sigh of relief, and continued down the hallway. She carefully closed the back door so it wouldn't slam, and then raced across the lawn.

When Chrissy reached the tree stump, she took off her necklace to fit the rock perfectly in the small hole on the surface. A silvery glow filled the evening light around it. Chrissy pulled on the leather of the necklace, opening the tree like a trapdoor. She took the rock out of the hole, put it back around her neck, and jumped in.

Chapter 10

*T*he last rays of pink sunlight arched across the sky, setting soft light on the Village of the Winglets. The sight of a circle of small cabins surrounding a huge, gleaming tree-house made Chrissy's heart leap for joy; she had been worried about what Luther might do . . . No, Chrissy told herself, don't think about that.

The problem was nobody seemed to be out. Chrissy wandered around, finally deciding to check the tree-house. She climbed up the ladder and opened the door, noticing that the handle was carved into a horse's head.

Inside, the whole village sat around a long table that had been prepared to seat about thirty. They were talking and eating and passing around large platters of food. Then, one person at the far end of the table noticed Chrissy and stood up. It was the Leader, Matthew, and his bright blue eyes were twinkling.

Matthew smiled at Chrissy, and then cleared his throat loudly. Alivia, who was sitting next to him, heard and looked up. She realized what was happening and started shushing her neighbors, until the whole table got quiet.

"Um . . . sorry to barge in," Chrissy said awkwardly. Then she grinned, "Is there any food left?"

"Of course!" Matthew replied, gesturing to the heaping platters around the table. "Welcome, Chrissy."

Chrissy sat down in the only empty chair, the head of the table across from Matthew. "Good, 'cause I'm starving!" She laughed and began eating. In the middle, Claudia stood up and came over to Chrissy. The people sitting next to her made room so that the two best friends could sit together and chat.

Once the meal was finished and the dishes were washed, everyone flooded out of the tree-house, bid each other good night, and began dispersing to their cabins. Chrissy had followed Claudia and now asked her, "Can I stay with you?"

"Oh, absolutely!" Claudia said, and led the way to her cabin.

Chrissy wearily followed Claudia into her bedroom. "You can take my bed, and I'll sleep on the couch," Claudia offered.

"No, no, no!" Chrissy insisted. "You can take your own bed. I'm so tired, I could fall asleep on the floor!"

"Okay," Claudia replied wearily, too tired to argue. She climbed into her bed and fell asleep immediately. Chrissy however, stayed awake on the couch, thinking. All this month, Chrissy had been having the same dream. Dancing at the edge of her thoughts appeared a necklace, made of wood on a silver chain. She tried to reach it, but Luther would always grab it away from her. She had no clue whose it was or where it came from, and Chrissy was tired of wondering why Luther wanted it. Exhausted, she fell asleep.

*　　*　　*

Darkness surrounded her. Dim light shone on trees all around. Ahead, she saw a clearing. Luther was standing in front of her. He seemed to be arguing with someone. Chrissy stepped forward, and she could see Lisa tied to a tree.

"Give it to me!" Luther was screeching.

"I don't have it," Lisa replied calmly.

"Yes you do! Give it, now!"

"I don't have it," Lisa insisted. Luther shouted some more. The two didn't seem to notice Chrissy. I must be dreaming, *she thought.* This is all a dream, and Lisa is okay, and Luther doesn't have her. *The world started to spin, and Chrissy tumbled into blackness.*

*   *   *

Chrissy woke up looking at fish and dolphins. After a moment of confusion, she realized two things: first, they were wood, and second, they were part of a table leg. Chrissy sat up, dazed. She had been sleeping on a wooden couch with baby blue cushions. In front of her stood the table carved with fish and dolphins. Then a light clicked on in her brain: Claudia's cabin.

Chrissy stood up and stretched. She heard something sizzling, and the smell of bacon wafted toward her. So, she followed her nose into the kitchen, where Claudia and her parents were already sitting at the table.

They introduced themselves. "I'm Michael."

"I'm Emma."

"G'morning," Chrissy said politely, trying not to sound as tired as she was.

"Someone's a late starter!" Claudia said brightly as she passed Chrissy a plate of scrambled eggs.

"Whattimeisit?" Chrissy asked groggily as she plopped into a chair.

"Time for the bacon to be ready," Emma responded briskly, getting up to check it.

"Mmm." Chrissy took a few more bites of egg.

"So," Claudia said. "How's Alexis doing?"

"Oh no!" Chrissy cried, dropping her fork and springing from the table. "I brought her—and Thunder—but I forgot all about them! I must have dropped them last night in the dark!" With that, Chrissy raced out the door.

"Wait!" Claudia called after her. "Who's Thunder?" She sighed, stood up and headed out to follow Chrissy.

Chrissy searched the cold, dewy grass for her wooden friends. She clonked her head against something, and discovered that she had wandered to the ladder of the tree-house. "Well," she said to herself, "I remember them being in my hand climbing up the ladder, but not when I came down. So they must be in the tree-house!"

Chrissy clambered up the ladder and opened the door. Inside, she was relieved to find that Alexis and Thunder were on the table right where Chrissy had stood them last night. At the far end of the table, Matthew was sitting, writing something and muttering to himself. He looked up and said brightly, "Good morning, Chrissy."

"Good morning, Matthew," Chrissy replied hastily as she grabbed Alexis and Thunder and exited the tree-house.

*　　*　　*

Back in Claudia's cabin, they sat on the couch in the living room, and the two horses stood on the table. "This is Thunder," Chrissy told Claudia. "He's one of Alexis's foals."

"One of?" Claudia asked.

"The other is named Lightning, but I haven't made her yet."

"Then let's make her now!" Claudia cried. She went to the locked drawer in the kitchen. After snapping the combination, Claudia took out two knives and the owl that she hadn't finished carving yet. Coming back into the living room, Claudia looked at Chrissy—"Well, you know the drill, go find your stick!"

While Chrissy went outside and searched, Claudia worked on her owl. Soon, Chrissy came back in with a thick piece of wood and sat down next to Claudia. She picked up her knife. Closing her eyes, Chrissy pictured Thunder and Lightning, two foals playing with each other, and started carving.

Claudia stopped her owl and stared at Chrissy. How skilled she was! And she wasn't even looking! Minutes passed.

Chrissy had been having a little trouble with the sides. She pictured a sleek white foal, but her knife wouldn't carve straight. Still, Chrissy kept her eyes shut. She ended the tail with a small curl, and then opened her eyes. Chrissy gasped; the horse was just as she pictured, except that it had wings. How can you try to carve a normal horse, but end up carving wings? But, Chrissy thought, it seems natural since real lightning bolts look like they're flying, in a sense, so why shouldn't the horse?

"Let's take them out!" Claudia cried. Chrissy scooped up all three horses and followed her into the small room with the basin. Chrissy remembered this as the room in which they had given Alexis life. The purple liquid still filled the basin. Chrissy dropped Thunder and Lightning into the basin and they sank to the bottom. They watched excitedly as the basin went through the same process of fizzing, clearing, and draining. Chrissy picked up the two foals and the girls ran outside.

This time, Chrissy knew exactly what to do. She put the three horses on the ground, a good distance apart. "Alexis, Thunder, Lightning!" she called.

They grew and grew and grew. Alexis, a fierce, pure-white mare, was tossing her mane proudly. Her two foals romped about next to her. Thunder was a spirited black foal full of energy, and Lightning was white like her mother, but with great golden wings and immense speed.

Chrissy pulled herself up onto Alexis's back, and Claudia onto Thunder's. They galloped around the village, laughing and playing. Then they started a game: Alexis and Thunder would run around and try to tag Lightning. They wove around the cabins, teaming up to *try* to corner Lightning. It was already difficult to catch up with her speed, but whenever they got close, Lightning would spread her wings and fly all the way to the other end of the circle.

After playing for hours, they finally lay exhausted in the grass. "I guess I should go home soon," Chrissy said sadly. "My mom'll be furious with me. C'mon Alexis, Thunder, Lightning." They shrank back into wood horses, and Chrissy scooped them up.

A voice behind them said, "Before you go, Chrissy, I'd like to do something for you." It was Matthew. The two girls followed him into a side room in his cabin, where he too had a basin of purple liquid. "May I see your necklace, Chrissy?" She took it off and handed it to him. "Now I ask that you please step out for a moment." They shuffled out of the room and closed the door behind them.

"Do you know what he's doing?"

"No, do you?"

"If I did, why would I be asking you?"

"I don't know!"

"Shhhhh! I hear something!"

Inside, they could hear Matthew mumbling, then chanting, getting louder and louder. There was a short silence for a moment. Suddenly a blinding flash of light blazed under the doorway, then blackness. Chrissy and Claudia looked cautiously at each other, and knocked on the door.

"Come in, girls," Matthew said. "It's okay."

They could see nothing different about the room. Matthew pointed at the basin. "You can get it back now." Chrissy looked in the basin and saw her necklace lying peacefully at the bottom. As she took it out, it dried immediately, and she put it around her neck. "That should help you with the situation with your mother," Matthew said, eyes twinkling. "You must go now."

"Yes," Chrissy agreed glumly. "Thanks Matthew, goodbye Claudia." She gave her friend a quick hug, and went outside.

As she slowly walked back to her tree, Chrissy thought about how fun this morning had been, and how she dreaded meeting her mother. Even her curiosity about what Matthew did with her necklace was overshadowed with anxiety. She leaned against the door of the tree, and it opened—back to her world.

Chapter 11

When Chrissy jumped out of the tree-stump, she saw the dreadful scene of her mom, lying in a lawn chair, waiting for Chrissy to appear. Chrissy knew her mom would suspect *something* was up with the tree, but she could never have even *imagined* what she was about to see.

At first, her mom looked startled, but then she jumped up and towered over Chrissy. "Go to your room," she ordered. Chrissy experienced a tingling sensation all over, and she knew just what to say.

"But we are in my room, Mom." She felt her neck grow hot, and Chrissy looked down. The rock on her necklace was glowing purple. Suddenly, the air around them shimmered, like heat waves on a hot day. The light bent, and the two found themselves in what appeared to be Chrissy's room.

Her mom's eyes glazed over, blinking a few times. "Right," she mumbled in a daze, and shuffled out the door.

Once her mom left, the air shimmered again, the light straightened, and Chrissy found herself still standing in the backyard. She could see her mom just going in the back door. "Wow," she breathed in amazement and relief. Chrissy sprinted joyfully across the lawn toward the house.

* * *

After lunch, Chrissy collapsed on her bed. What a wonderful day it had been so far, and she didn't even get in trouble for it! Then she remembered what Lisa had said yesterday afternoon: "I'll send someone to check in with you by tomorrow night." Chrissy told herself not to worry, for it was only the afternoon.

A couple of minutes later, Chrissy's mom wandered in. Her eyes had refocused, but she looked like she really didn't want to say what she was about to say. "I've been thinking," she started, "and I feel it was . . . unfair of me to ground you for a . . . small thing like that. So . . . you're not grounded anymore."

"Yes!" Chrissy jumped up and hugged her mom, who patted her back awkwardly and left quickly. Chrissy was still rejoicing when her dad called her to dinner.

*　　*　　*

Chrissy had a wonderful dinner and a dream-free sleep, and she woke up perfectly happy until about halfway through her bowl of cereal. Suddenly remembering Lisa and her messenger, Chrissy dropped her spoon with a clatter and sprinted to her room.

Something was wrong. Lisa had never sent her messenger! Chrissy had to go to the Winglets and tell them what she knew. She hurriedly got dressed and put her necklace on. She decided she needed a backpack and threw in Alexis, Thunder, Lightning, a flashlight, and a pocket knife. Chrissy rummaged in her desk drawer for a sheet of paper to write a note to her parents, but something new brushed against her hand.

Grabbing it to pull it out, Chrissy was surprised to see a small wood symbol on a silver chain. It was the same necklace from Chrissy's dreams! Something told her that this was Lisa's necklace, the one that her parents had given her, the one she had hidden. So that's what she was doing in Chrissy's room that day! She had hidden the gift from her parents with Chrissy!

Worry washed over Chrissy as she realized what her dream might mean; Luther did want to take the necklace. Fear came next; what about the second dream, where Luther had captured Lisa, enraged that she didn't have her necklace? It fit though. Lisa didn't send her messenger. What if Chrissy's dreams were telling her something? And without the necklace to protect Lisa from Luther's anger . . . Chrissy shuddered, and stuffed the necklace in with the rest of her supplies.

Chrissy shouldered her backpack and ran outside, hoping that nobody would see her. Breathless, she barely paid attention to what she was doing as she put the key in the lock and opened the door in the tree stump. Chrissy took one last look at her house, and then jumped in to save her friend.

Chapter 12

Chrissy could barely tell where she was. The sky was bleak and gray. The tree-house had been burned to the ground, as had several of the cabins. Chrissy cautiously walked into the Village, staring at the wreckage.

She gave a start when one of the cabin doors opened behind her. Chrissy whirled around and saw Claudia, pale and frightened, in the doorway. "Are you CRAZY? Get in here, hurry!"

Chrissy rushed inside and Claudia slammed the door behind her. The two friends hugged each other, relieved. "Let's go downstairs," Claudia suggested.

Chrissy went down the steps and into the basement, where Claudia's parents were already sitting. When the two girls entered, Michael stood up. "Chrissy, it's not safe for you here."

"Neither for you!" Chrissy said stubbornly. "Anyway, I've come to help you. I know what Luther is after-"

"He already found it," Michael said sadly. "Luther has captured Lisa."

"He wasn't looking for Lisa," Chrissy insisted, setting her backpack down and rummaging through it. "He's looking for this!" She held up Lisa's necklace. Claudia and her parents looked terrified.

Suddenly, they heard someone pounding on the door. Michael stood up and bravely went to get it. The rest sat in silence, waiting. When Michael came back down he said quietly, "They need you too, Emma."

"Mom, don't go!" Claudia cried. Her mom hugged her.

"It'll be okay," she whispered. "I have to go." Claudia let go of her mother and watched them slowly walk up the steps.

Silence again. Minutes dragged by. Finally, Chrissy said, "We have to find Lisa. She's our only hope." Claudia quietly agreed, and the two went up and outside.

Once out of the cabin, Chrissy started walking briskly toward the forest. She looked back and saw that Claudia was lagging behind. "I'm scared," Claudia whispered.

"Don't be," Chrissy told her. Her necklace glowed purple, the air shimmered, and they were standing in sunlight. The tree-house and all the cabins gleamed perfectly, and Alexis, Thunder, and Lightning were prancing behind them.

Claudia looked at all this, swallowed, and said, "Let's do this." Chrissy held the illusion until they were at the edge of the forest, then they were plunged into darkness.

*   *   *

Chrissy tried to remember where Luther had taken her when she was kidnapped. That had been a month ago, they were in pitch blackness, and they had the promise of nothing good ahead. So, basically, they were completely lost.

Something big moved ahead of them. Claudia clutched Chrissy's arm. "What was *that?*"

"I don't know," Chrissy replied anxiously. Suddenly, Chrissy could've kicked herself. "Oh! I forgot, I have a flashlight in my backpack!" She dug around, pulled out her flashlight, and flicked it on, straight into the pale, leering face of Luther Rehtul.

Chapter 13

A dozen more men appeared out of the shadows, forming a circle. They were surrounded.

The flashlight dropped out of Chrissy's hand, and it went out. She heard Luther's steely voice, "Bind the other one, and take her away."

"No!" Chrissy cried, and stumbled to her left, in the direction she *thought* Claudia was standing. Claudia, on Chrissy's right, gave a shriek of terror as three pairs of hands seized her and pulled her away. Chrissy found herself pushed forward toward Luther.

Luther grabbed Chrissy's shoulders and pulled her along. "Chrissy, my friend! Long time no see!" Chrissy started to growl something in response, but stopped as they came into a little clearing lit by one small lantern.

Luther stood Chrissy at the edge of the clearing and released her. Immediately, three burly men stationed themselves behind and on either side of her. Luther called, "Bring in my dear little sister!"

Lisa stepped into the clearing, flanked and followed by guards. When she saw Chrissy, Lisa moaned. "No! The desk . . . ?" Chrissy gave a tiny nod, and Lisa gave a wail of despair and dropped to her knees. The guards pulled her roughly to her feet.

"Oh! So you do know each other!" Luther said. "I figured . . ." Suddenly, he threw his hands in the air, shouting, "Muli!"

Thick white walls materialized around the clearing, trapping them in. Then Luther snapped his fingers, and the guards disappeared. The girls were alone with Luther, who turned to Chrissy and said in a falsely bright voice, "Now then! It was quite fortunate that I had a piece of Lasceri with me to make a duplicate of your 'key' that time I had it, a long month ago. It became most helpful when I came here to check on my forces, did it not? Otherwise, I would not have come upon dear Lisa, sneaking through the woods." Luther sneered menacingly at Lisa, and turned back to Chrissy. "I'd have thought that you would be looking for me in your own world after seeing me there, but apparently not." Lisa looked questioningly at Chrissy. Luther continued, "Anyway, down to business. There is a certain necklace that you have and I want. But we'll deal with that later. I have some things to do first."

Luther walked over to a small tree-stump, lifted his arms, and began to chant. As he chanted, the temperature rose and their walled clearing grew steadily hotter. The air became heavy with electricity. Chrissy felt herself getting dizzy.

Luther stopped chanting, and put his arms down. Suddenly, a flash of light bolted toward the stump and a jagged block of obsidian appeared. "The connection stone!" Chrissy heard Lisa whisper, eyes wide and fear in her voice. From what Chrissy could see, a small hole had been cut on either end of it. Luther, meanwhile, had taken off one of his rings. It was made of gold and had the same symbol as Lisa's necklace. Behind the symbol, the ring was set with a ruby. Luther fit his ring in the hole on the left side of the obsidian. The heat intensified, the electricity doubled. Chrissy promptly passed out.

Chrissy dreamed that she was flying. Great golden wings beat steadily on either side of her. She was about to look down to see what she was riding on when she got roughly shaken awake.

"Get up, girl!" Luther barked. "Stand up! *Now!*" Chrissy pushed herself back to her feet and looked around, dazed. She was still in the forest, sweating from heat, and wishing she was still flying through the cool night air. Luther's voice was dangerously soft. "Now, just give me the necklace."

Chrissy's head was still spinning, but she had an idea. She took off her backpack, opened it up, and carefully spilled its contents on the ground. Luther sneered at the pocket knife and three wood horses, but he stared hungrily at the necklace Chrissy was now picking up.

"Yes . . . yes . . . that's it . . . just give it to me now."

"Don't listen to him!" Lisa cried.

"Stay out of this, you foolish sister!" Luther spat. "Now, GIVE IT TO ME!" He lunged at Chrissy, trying to pry it from her grasp.

While Luther wrestled for the necklace, Chrissy cried, "Alexis, Thunder, Lightning!" The three horses sprang to life and charged. Thunder galloped over to Lisa, who pulled herself onto his back. Lightning knocked Luther over, and Chrissy tried to climb up, but Luther sprang back, finally managing to wrench the necklace from her hand. He ran over to the connection stone. The necklace was millimeters away from being in the hole when Alexis reared, causing Luther to duck out of the way.

Alexis's right hoof pounded on the center of the connection stone, and it cracked in pieces. The air around the clearing exploded, dropping twenty degrees. The walls crumbled around them and disappeared. Lightning crackled around the obsidian, and Alexis had to jump out of the way. Luther was thrown backward and landed on his back a couple feet away.

Chrissy trotted over on Lightning to where Luther was lying. She plucked the necklace from his hand. "What is it with you and stealing people's necklaces?" she asked grimly.

They went over to where Lisa and Thunder were waiting, and Alexis joined them. "I believe this is yours," Chrissy said, handing the necklace to Lisa.

"Thanks," she stammered, and she put it around her neck. As Chrissy scooped up the contents of her backpack and put it on, the obsidian disappeared with a wave of Lisa's hand.

Chapter 14

*L*ightning spread her wings and took off into the air. The sky was brightening to be a wonderful afternoon. "This is just how it was in my dream," Chrissy thought, "only much, much, better!" She looked down and saw Alexis, Lisa and Thunder galloping through the trees below them.

Soon, they came to the edge of the forest. Chrissy noticed that the tree-house and all the cabins were beautifully restored. The three down below had stopped, so Lightning circled lower and lower, finally landing on the ground near them. Then Chrissy saw why they had stopped—Claudia was lying on the ground, tied up in thick ropes.

Chrissy slipped off Lightning's back and ran over to Claudia. She dropped to her knees and dug around in her backpack, finally producing her pocket knife. She flicked it open and began quickly and carefully cutting the ropes that bound her friend. During these few tense minutes, Chrissy caught Claudia up on what had happened. Once all the ropes had been cut, Claudia stood up, rubbing her wrists and stretching. "Oh, that feels good. Thank you so much, Chrissy. I was beginning to wonder . . ."

They all mounted their horses and cantered into the village, pounding on doors and shouting for joy. Claudia's parents hugged Claudia tightly. "Luther's men took us away so we wouldn't interfere with what Luther would do," her mom explained. "Luther knew you would come to help Lisa once we left, and that we wouldn't let you go alone, so he made us leave. Once his enchantments broke, everything disappeared, and we could come back! Thank you!"

Soon, the whole village was assembled in the grass in front of the tree-house. Chrissy saw Lisa and Matthew slip out of the crowd and head to Matthew's cabin, but she didn't say anything. Then she told the Winglets everything—her dreams, what Lisa told her, and the episode in the woods. She paused to catch her breath.

Suddenly, Chrissy gasped, and the crowd turned to look; Lisa had come out of Matthew's cabin, utterly transformed. She had a magnificent green and turquoise gown with a trailing white cloak lined with fur. Her necklace gleamed around her neck. She looked tall, proud, and queenly as she strode over to the crowd.

"I am Lisa," she proclaimed, "Enchantress of the age, and Leader of the old ways, now the new ways." The crowd cheered, and Lisa smiled. "After the fire many years ago, I fled into Chrissy's world. Thankfully, she found her way into our world. Here, Claudia inspired Chrissy and helped create these fine horses who aided us greatly. Therefore I must thank Chrissy and Claudia for their help in foiling Luther's plans, and of course the horses too!" she added. Alexis, standing nearby with her foals, whinnied. "Chrissy's bravery and wit have proven truly powerful." The village applauded for Chrissy, who blushed.

"It's my dreams," she told them. "They show me what's going to happen."

"Yes," Lisa agreed. "Dreams often tell you things, even about the future. You should listen to them.

"I would also like to explain the connection stone my brother tried to use this morning. It is made of obsidian, and used to hold two very powerful magical objects and combine their power. I have not found a way to destroy the pieces, but they have been scattered all over the world in protected places, not able to be summoned by magic. There have been charms placed on them to make them undetectable. There are over thirty pieces, and all of them are needed to reconnect its power, so Luther will have quite a job collecting them.

"Now enough talk, let us celebrate the new ways with a feast!"

Up until now, Chrissy hadn't noticed how hungry she was, but now she realized that she was starving.

*   *   *

After lunch, Chrissy sat down with Lisa. "Are we just going to let Luther go?" Chrissy asked.

"If I know my brother, he'll have something else in mind, but I've put protections on the Winglets so that he can't enter the village."

"That's good. Do you have any idea of what he might do, where he might go?"

"My brother has always been unpredictable, but if you ever need me," she gestured around, "I'll be here. But *you* have to go to school tomorrow."

"Oh, come on! You're fourteen! You have to go to school tomorrow too!" Chrissy cried.

"I'm twenty-two."

"You said yourself you're fourteen!"

"I'm twenty-two."

"Fourteen!"

"Twenty-two!"

"Fourteen!"

"Girls, is there a problem?" Matthew had come over.

"Oh, no I just . . ." Chrissy glanced sheepishly at Lisa. "I think I should go home now."

"Okay, well, just grab your things and we'll see you off," he replied.

Chrissy collected her backpack and called her horses back to wood. She walked up to the tree, and turned around for a last look at the village. The people were wandering around having a good time. She called to them "Goodbye everyone! Good luck with The Ways!"

Claudia ran over to give her one last hug. Content, Chrissy disappeared through the tree, back to her world.

To Robyn Little-

my amazing fourth grade teacher who took a
personal interest in my writing from the start

Part 3

Beneath the Surface

Chapter 15

A small ball of blue light appeared through the pitch blackness. Lit by the light of the ball was a face, pale and grimacing. As the ball of light grew, more things came into view. The face belonged to a man, wearing tiger skins and many rings. A blurry figure was standing across from the man. He looked remarkably like the first man, except silvery, translucent, and older.

The older man looked furious, and the younger one acted like a child in trouble. The older man was speaking. "This does not please me."

"No, Father," the younger one whimpered.

"I will not accept any more mistakes."

"No, Father."

"You cost us precious time."

"I know, Father."

"Stop saying that! It was handed to you like you were a child but you still couldn't do the job!"

The younger one said nothing. Then the father's voice became dangerously soft. "You're in luck, Son. There is another way. It will take much longer, and you are wasting my precious energy, but we might still be able to pull this off."

"Thank you Father."

The world started spinning into darkness as the ball of light was extinguished. All senses were overwhelmed by a feeling of falling through space and time . . .

Chapter 16

Chrissy woke with a start and sat up to look around. She was still in her own bed, in her own room. There were no dark, unknown places, no evil men.

Chrissy breathed a sigh of relief, and then she remembered: Today is February eighteenth, my birthday! She jumped out of bed and quickly got dressed into jeans, a tye-dye t-shirt, smiley-face earrings, and of course her rock necklace that she wore everywhere.

Chrissy ran downstairs to the kitchen, but . . . nobody was there. "Oh, right," she remembered glumly. "It's Friday. I have to go to school."

*　　*　　*

At recess, Chrissy's friend Amanda skipped over to where Chrissy was hanging out under the big maple tree next to the playground. "Happy Birthday!" she said brightly as she stopped next to Chrissy.

"Thanks. I'm so excited about tonight; my family's going to go out to dinner. I'm twelve today!"

"You're lucky, mine's not 'till May. Oh yeah, here." Amanda took a piece of paper out of her pocket and handed it to Chrissy.

Chrissy opened up a brightly colored birthday card covered in glitter. "Oh, it's so pretty! Thanks a lot!"

For the rest of the day, Chrissy could barely pay attention to what the teachers said; she was so excited for her birthday plans. When she finally got home, Chrissy ran off the bus to her house and dumped her backpack in the hallway. She skipped into the kitchen, where a large pile of brightly colored packages were stacked precariously on the table. A note in front of the stack read:

You can open the small one on top.
We will be home at 4.

Chrissy looked at the top of the stack and took down a small, sparkly green, square package. She tore off the paper and opened the box. Inside were two earrings. One was a s'more, and the other was a campfire. Chrissy immediately swapped her smiley-faces for the new pair. Then she noticed another small piece of paper tucked in the bottom. It said:

The backyard, 9 o'clock.

Chrissy smiled; s'mores! Her favorite dessert! She itched to open more presents, but she finally tried to read a book instead.

*   *   *

Chrissy was nearly bored to death by four o'clock, but eventually her parents and her brothers, Russ and Alex, came home. "There's the birthday girl!" her mom announced cheerfully, setting down the groceries on the table and hugging Chrissy. Looking over her mother's shoulder, Chrissy could see graham-crackers and marshmallows sticking out of the bag.

"Happy birthday Chrissy!" her dad said. He tapped her earrings. "I hope you like your earrings; Alex picked them out for you."

"Yes, and it took *such* a long time to find them," Alex said with fake exhaustion. "But I kept looking, *just* for you."

"Oh, it seems to have absolutely *drained* you of your energy," Chrissy said sarcastically. Russ popped his present on top of the pile.

As Chrissy's mom unpacked the groceries, her dad said, "How about you open your presents now, then we'll go out to dinner and come back for some s'mores. How does that sound?"

"Great!" Chrissy answered, plopping herself into the chair in front of the pile, which towered over her. As her family settled into chairs around table, she selected a bright blue, oblong present from the top, and shook it. Something rattled inside. Tearing off the paper, she revealed a set of art supplies, including paints, paintbrushes, a canvas, a palette, and pencils. "Oh, I love it!" she cried.

Next she picked a red bag with balloons on it, containing an earring tree shaped like a butterfly. After that came a sparkly yellow box with a set of books in it. A small envelope contained a gift card to Target, and a rather squishy purple bag had a colorful new pillow. In a small green package was the new movie Chrissy had been talking about for weeks.

The last present was a flat blue box with "Happy Birthday" written all over it that held new clothes.

"Thank you so much!" Chrissy cried, hugging her parents. By now, everyone started getting hungry, so they decided to go out to dinner. Chrissy picked her favorite restaurant, and they had a wonderful time.

Once they got back from dinner, Chrissy's parents prepared for s'mores and Russ and Alex started the campfire in the backyard. Chrissy sat in her snow-throne they had built, watching them. Soon, her dad came out with five marshmallow skewers. Her mom followed, carrying a tray of graham crackers, chocolate, and a bag of marshmallows. They set them down near the fire pit and handed Chrissy one marshmallow on a skewer.

Once it was toasted to perfection and all assembled into a s'more, her mom stuck a candle in the crack of the top cracker and lit it. They sang "Happy Birthday," and Chrissy blew out the candle. She pulled it out and took a huge bite of her s'more. Marshmallow squished out the edges, making her fingers messy, exactly the way she liked it.

Soon, everyone was either roasting marshmallows or eating a s'more. Chrissy, Russ, and Alex were competing to see who got their fingers/face the marshmallowiest. So far, the only finger Chrissy had without marshmallow on it was her right pinky, and Alex had somehow gotten some on his nose. It had been a great night, but they had to scrub their fingers and faces for *forever* to get all the goo off.

At last, they sat on the couch to watch Chrissy's new movie. Once it ended, Chrissy got into her pajamas, exhausted but happy. As she climbed into bed, she remembered her scary dream from last night, with the two men. Most people would think, "Oh, thank goodness it was only a dream," but Chrissy knew better. Just last week she learned that her dreams really reveal the future.

While trying to get to sleep, thoughts floated through her mind. In the last visit to the Winglet world, Chrissy had dreamt about her old enemy, Luther. In her dream, he had captured Lisa and wanted the necklace that Lisa had received as a gift from their parents, but she had hidden it with Chrissy. Chrissy soon realized that Lisa was missing, confirming that her dream had actually happened.

Chrissy set out to rescue Lisa, but ended up getting caught herself. Luther tried to use the obsidian connection stone to combine the power of their parents' gifts, but Chrissy wrecked his plans. Chrissy dreamed that she was flying, which helped her realize a way to escape by calling her horses. Alexis cracked the connection stone, destroying Luther's magic so that they could return to the village. There, Lisa resumed leading the Winglets as their enchantress. Chrissy had been reluctant to return to her world, but she knew the Winglets were safe with Lisa.

All that happened last weekend. This had been an uneventful week so far, which meant it was boring, dull, and exasperatingly normal. The most exciting thing that had happened this week (other than her birthday) was the dream, and although it was somewhat exciting, it scared her. She recognized the younger man as Luther, but what about the other figure, whom Luther had called "Father?" Chrissy remembered Lisa saying that Luther was her brother, and that their parents had turned to evil ways. She didn't mention what had happened to them, though. Chrissy assumed that their father must be a ghost, for he didn't seem fully solid.

Since tomorrow was the weekend, Chrissy decided to visit the Winglets in the morning and tell them about her dream. With that thought, she finally fell into an uneasy but dreamless sleep.

*   *   *

Chrissy woke up early the next morning and scarfed down her breakfast. Once she raced back upstairs to get dressed and make her bed, she grabbed Alexis, Thunder, and Lightning off her bedside table. As soon as she was ready, Chrissy slipped lightly back down the steps so that she wouldn't wake up her parents. She was tying her shoelaces when Russ and Alex came down the steps. "Where are you going?" Russ asked.

"Just . . . walking around the neighborhood. What's wrong with that?" Alex raised his eyebrows suspiciously. Chrissy hurried out the door.

Chrissy ducked behind the house and into the backyard. Walking to the tree-stump, Chrissy took off her rock necklace. She fit it into the small hole on the surface of the stump, and silvery light glowed around the edges. Chrissy pulled on the leather loop of her necklace and the old stump creaked open like a trapdoor. She picked out her rock, put it back around her neck, and jumped in.

*   *   *

The familiar sight of cabins circling the big tree-house welcomed Chrissy warmly. She raced into the clearing and went to one of the cabins. She knocked on the door calling,

"Hello, Claudia! It's me, Chrissy! I have important news . . . hello?"

When Claudia didn't answer her door, Chrissy went over to Matthew's cabin. He didn't answer either, so Chrissy checked the tree-house. Nobody was inside. "Where *could* they all be?" Chrissy wondered. "I don't think-"

Suddenly, a loud cheer shattered her thoughts as the whole village sprang from various hiding places around the clearing shouting, "Happy Birthday Chrissy!" They surged toward her and hugged her.

"How did you guys know?" Chrissy exclaimed in surprise. Lisa just smiled in her annoyingly silent way.

Once everyone had settled down, Claudia presented Chrissy with a full set of carving tools. Chrissy was delighted. Claudia also informed her that she had finished the owl carving she had started a while ago. "His name is Chase," she said.

Next Lisa gave her a charm bracelet with three charms, one for Alexis, Thunder, and Lightning. "You can hold them each in their charm, so you won't have to carry them and they'll always be with you," she told Chrissy.

Chrissy looked relieved, because she had nowhere to put her three horses who were lying in the grass right now. Lisa instructed Chrissy on how to put them away, and Chrissy repeated the incantation Lisa told her. Light collected around the wooden carvings, blocking them from view. When it cleared, the horses were gone, and Chrissy's bracelet felt warm. She stared at the intricate charms, and they seemed to glow.

"Thanks so much everybody!" she said, hugging Lisa. Then she whispered in Lisa's ear, "We need to talk."

Lisa understood, and called to the crowd, "We have some important matters to discuss, so you can go back to whatever you were doing! Thank you!" Soon the three of them strolled over to Lisa's cabin, newly built next to Matthew's.

"Nice cabin," Chrissy said as she entered Lisa's home. "You guys built this pretty quick, I only left last week!"

"Thanks," Lisa said proudly. She led them into the dining room, and Chrissy and Claudia sat down. Then Lisa went off to fix hot chocolate.

"Mmmm." That was all Chrissy could say about this wonderful hot chocolate. It was smooth and sweet and tasted of chocolate and vanilla and candy all blended together in a mouthwatering mixture.

"So . . . what did you need to talk about?" Lisa prompted.

Chrissy jerked out of her chocolate heaven. "Oh . . . right. I had this dream. I think Luther was in the woods, and there was a man with him. I think he was a ghost, but Luther kept calling him 'Father.'" Lisa listened more intently.

"What did he say?"

"Something about not being pleased, and that Luther had wasted precious time . . . and then he said something about there being another way . . . but he never said what."

"He never really was pleased about much," Lisa muttered. "Anything else?"

"Nope, that was pretty much it." Lisa sat back, lost in thought.

Suddenly, Claudia blurted, "We could look for him right away! Maybe he's in the forest of . . . Minia?"

"Minakia," Lisa corrected.

"But what about my parents?" Chrissy asked. "They'll be worried . . . or angry . . . but probably both."

"You're right," Lisa answered firmly. "We'll need a plan."

"Oh . . . right, a plan." Claudia hoped she was included in the "we."

The three discussed how Chrissy was going to deal with her family, what they should pack, and where they should start looking for Luther. At about ten, the meeting ended. "Right," Lisa concluded. "We'll leave tomorrow morning. Meeting adjourned." They stepped out into the sunlight.

Matthew greeted them by the door. "Is everything okay?" he asked.

"I'll tell you later," Lisa told him.

"I think I should leave now," Chrissy decided. "I need to get some things done. We've got an important day ahead of us!"

*   *   *

Chrissy walked in the door, took her shoes off, and went downstairs. She sat down and logged onto the computer. Pulling up a PowerPoint presentation, she carefully created an ad and printed it out, then folded it in three and addressed it. The plan was set, and everything was ready. Chrissy went upstairs to have lunch.

Stage 1: The Ploy

Chrissy waited patiently for lunch to be over. Then she jumped up from the table and cried, "I'll get the mail for you, Mom!"

Her mother looked surprised. "Oh . . . thank you, honey," but Chrissy was already out the door.

Chrissy came back in, pretending to look through the various bills, magazines and letters. Then she extracted her ad. "I wonder what this is . . ." Chrissy looked it over one more time, handed it to her mom and said, "It's for you."

"What is it?" Her mom scanned the page. "Hmmm . . ."

"What does it say?" Alex asked, puzzled.

"To: Residents of Greenwood, Colorado," she read aloud. "*This week only, enjoy a four-day, two-person suite at any ski resort in Greenwood, only $199! Book your stay now, before it's too late!* Wow, two hundred? That's pretty cheap."

"It actually sounds great, Mom. You and Dad could use a vacation," Alex said.

"But leaving you three alone for four days? We'd come home to find the house burned down!"

"Nah, we'll throw Chrissy in the closet and have a party!" Russ chimed in. Chrissy punched him.

"Really, you should go, Mom. We'll be fine," Chrissy insisted.

"Yeah, we'll keep this one in line." Alex cracked his knuckles and grinned at Chrissy.

"Oh, I don't know . . ."

"Come *on* Mom! You *love* skiing and it'll be just the two of you! Do it." Chrissy looked at the ad again. "It also ends tomorrow."

Their mother looked flustered, but she replied, "Alright, I'll talk it over with your Father."

"Right then, Russ," Alex said briskly, rubbing his hands together. "We should go figure out who to invite to the party." The two boys disappeared up the stairs. Chrissy followed them up and plopped on her bed.

Chrissy reviewed her progress. She had made the ad, her mom had seen it, and her mom was about to give in and go on the trip. Now all she had to do was get to the Winglets and stay for a few days without Russ or Alex knowing she was gone. Lisa and Claudia hadn't discussed that in their meeting, but left it for Chrissy to figure out. She thought for a while, and then came up with her best idea yet.

Outside, Chrissy found a good-sized stick and brought it in. Back in her room, she took out the carving tools that Claudia had given her and sat down on her bed. Now Chrissy imagined herself, a tall, red-haired, freckly twelve-year-old ready for an adventure.

Keeping this image in mind, Chrissy started carving into the wood, paying extra attention to details like eyes, hair, and fingers. It took longer than the horses had, but she needed this to be as accurate as possible. A few minutes later, she looked upon her carving. It was a mini-Chrissy, almost an exact replica. Chrissy was very proud.

Going into a drawer in her dresser, Chrissy pulled out leather pouch. It tingled and warmed her hand. Opening it revealed a small amount of purple liquid Claudia had given to her before she left. "It's called leximer," she had said. "A magical substance used for cleansing. It also has healing and life-giving properties—just in case."

Now Chrissy snuck into the kitchen, pulled a small bowl from the cabinets, and rushed back up to her room. Chrissy locked her door behind her and set the bowl on the dresser. Pouring some of the leximer into the bowl, she dropped in the carving of her miniature self. The leximer gurgled wildly, then stopped. The liquid turned from its purplish color to as clear as water, revealing at the bottom not a wood figure but an image of Chrissy herself. After a little bit, the image faded, and the purple leximer swirled around the bowl, slowly disappearing.

Chrissy took her figure out of the bowl and set it on the floor. Then, feeling a little foolish about calling herself, she called, "Chrissy!" The little statue on the floor grew rapidly. To Chrissy, it was like watching a flower bloom and grow, except all sped up. The statue was up to her knee, then her chest, then her chin, and finally stopped at Chrissy's exact height.

It was like looking into a 3-D mirror. Had someone looked into that room and saw the two Chrissies studying each other, they would have thought they had gone crazy, or Chrissy had moved her mirror, or they'd have just blinked a few times and fainted. But nobody walked into the room, and the two studied each other intently.

Chrissy Jr. spoke first. "Hello." She had Chrissy's exact voice.

"Hey," Chrissy said awkwardly.

"This is weird," Chrissy Jr. said, voicing Chrissy's thoughts. They both turned to face the actual mirror. Now there were four Chrissies standing in the room!

The real Chrissy sat down on the bed, eyes wide. "I would've said cool, but yeah, weird is more like it." Chrissy Jr. sat on the bed next to her.

"So . . . I'd sorta like to know why I'm here."

"Oh, right. I have to go somewhere, and I need you to stay here and make sure that my brothers, Russ and Alex, don't know that I'm gone."

"Sounds easy enough. What about your parents?"

"They'll be on vacation for four days. Hopefully I'll be back by then, but I have no idea how long this is going to take."

"Okay. Is that it?"

"Yep, I leave tomorrow morning."

"Great!"

Chapter 17

Chrissy waved to her parents as they backed out of the driveway and drove away. It had taken a lot to convince them that yes, they should get a vacation and yes, Russ and Alex would take care of her and no, they wouldn't burn the house down or throw a party or anything like that.

When they were gone, Chrissy trotted upstairs to pack her backpack. She put in some clothes, her toothbrush and toothpaste, a hairbrush, a flashlight, and a knife. Next, in went the leather pouch of leximer. She took her wood mini-self and went downstairs. She grabbed a water bottle from the fridge and stuffed it in her backpack.

"I'm going for a walk," Chrissy told Russ and Alex, who were eating breakfast at the table. Fortunately, they did not see the clothes in her backpack and didn't question her.

Stage 2: Departure

Chrissy left the house and circled around to the back. Then she took out Chrissy Jr., called her, and told her, "You might want to wait a little bit before going inside because they think I'm taking a walk."

"Alright."

"Bye, thanks, and good luck!" Chrissy walked over to the tree-stump. She slipped off her necklace. Fitting it into the hole, the silvery light swirled around her. Chrissy opened the tree and put her necklace back on. She adjusted her backpack and jumped in.

*   *   *

The village people were assembled in the clearing, waiting to see the girls off on their journey. After Chrissy brought the three horses out of her bracelet, they whinnied occasionally, standing nearby. The children loved to pet them.

Lisa appeared out of her cabin, settling a leather satchel on her side. She stood beside Chrissy at the front of the group, and waited as Claudia slung her bag over her shoulder and hurried over. Then Matthew moved forward and gave a blessing over their journey.

Once he was finished, Chrissy hoisted herself onto Lightning's back, Lisa to Alexis, and Claudia to Thunder. The village chorused good-byes and good lucks as they started riding north into the woods.

Stage 3: Unknown

After a few minutes, they found a narrow footpath that the Winglets used every few months to get to the marketplace. They chatted idly about whatever came to their minds.

A while later, Claudia looked at the compass she brought and remarked, "The path is veering slightly northwest, and if we want to get to the forest of Minakia according to the plan, we should break off northeast somewhere around here."

"You're right," Chrissy agreed. "Maybe someone should fly up with Lightning and try to scout around up there, to see about where to break off."

"I think you should do it," Lisa told Chrissy quickly.

"Well," Claudia reasoned, "Lisa knows the land best."

"No, Luther might be looking for me. I shouldn't go or I might be spotted," Lisa replied.

"Okay . . ." Chrissy was a little hesitant, but she went up anyway.

Wind rushing through her ears, Chrissy and Lightning rose to a tremendous height. Looking down, she saw a thin brown line snaking through the great green sea of trees. *That's the path we're on,* she thought. Far ahead, a cluster of buildings marked the marketplace. Slightly to her right, the jumble of different trees gave way to an even larger and older forest of giant pine trees. *That has got to be the forest of Minakia.* She looked along the path and spotted a great fallen log. *We'll just reach that log and turn sharply right, then keep going until we reach the pines.* It wasn't the most direct route, but they wanted to stick to the path as long as possible, for they only had enough food to last a few days and getting lost in the woods is *not* fun.

*   *   *

After arriving at the log and traveling to the right for a while, Claudia suddenly cried, "I see one! There's a pine tree! We're almost there!" Lisa looked where Claudia pointed and sure enough, there was a pine tree. Soon they saw dozens of them as far as the eye could see. It was somewhat of a relief, because each of them had been silently thinking that Chrissy might have misjudged and they were way off track.

When they passed a small creek at the border of the two forests, they stopped and gave the horses a drink and a break. While the girls had sandwiches and refilled their waters, Lisa gave each of the horses an apple from her satchel. After the break, they packed up and kept going.

Once they were deep in the forest of Minakia, Chrissy noticed an unnatural silence, quite different from the loud, lively, chatter of animals and birds in the other forest. "Why is it so quiet?" she found herself whispering.

"The Quopes have placed spells to keep things out of this part of their woods; they don't like interruptions. And I shudder to wonder if they already know we're here," Lisa explained.

"Oh . . ." Claudia stopped. "We shouldn't just walk around aimlessly until they find us. Where are we going to look for Luther?"

"When he was here last he stayed with Blockhead's family village, so maybe we should look there first."

"There's a whole village for one family?" Chrissy asked.

"Yes, they are very large families and each has their own private village. They are *very* big on privacy. The Great Minakia Feast is the only time they all come together, gathered in the biggest village, once a year. They even have a competition to see whose village is the best to host the feast. It is a great family honor to host it."

"Do you know where Blockhead's village is?"

"Not exactly . . . oh look! There's part of one! Do you see that cabin there?"

They looked, and Lisa was right. Up ahead, they could see the back of a cabin, part of a Quope village. They couldn't see any lights on, but they stopped well away from it anyway while Lisa decided what to do. "I'm going to go over there and check it out. You two stay here, in case I get caught." They seemed uneasy, but Lisa never specified what to do if she *did* get caught.

Chrissy watched Lisa creep away silently toward the cabins. When she reached the back of one of them, she leaned against it and took a deep breath. Then she sidled along to the edge and peered around. After a few tense moments, she edged around the corner and disappeared from view.

The two girls waited in nervous silence, straining their ears to hear anything coming from the village. After staring at the same spot for several minutes, Chrissy noticed the light was slowly dwindling. Looking up at the sky, she figured that it had to be at least five. They should find somewhere to rest soon, because there was already little light in this dense forest and they would get nowhere in the dark.

Suddenly, Lisa popped out from behind the cabin and ran lightly toward them. "It's completely empty!" she told them with glee. "I don't know why, but there's absolutely no one there, and we've *got* to take advantage of this. There might not be another village for miles."

"I was just noticing it's getting dark. This would be a perfect place to have dinner and get some rest," Chrissy remarked. Claudia agreed, so they made their way through the trees toward the village.

Walking around the one cabin they could see, Chrissy found herself in a village similar to the Winglets'. There were six cabins clustered together, circling a large fire pit. Each cabin looked dark and foreboding, as well as cold and empty. The forest seemed even darker now, and Chrissy shivered, whether from cold or fear she couldn't tell.

They decided to sleep off to the right of the fire pit. Chrissy arranged a thick bed of pine needles for them. Claudia brought out three blankets from her bag and laid them on the needles. It was about as good as they could get.

Chrissy sat on the edge of their makeshift bed, and munched on some of the carrots Lisa gave her. Claudia sat down beside her and took some too. They shared a couple of sips from Chrissy's water bottle. Lisa went over and fed the horses some sugar cubes. Nobody really felt like doing anything. Finally Chrissy stood up and called to the horses. They shrank into wood. She recited the spell and they glowed momentarily. In a few seconds, they were safely inside Chrissy's charm bracelet.

Chrissy and Claudia went to bed early out of sheer boredom. Lisa, however, stayed up long into the night, pacing.

*　　*　　*

Chrissy woke up early, body aching. She noticed that Lisa and Claudia were still sleeping, so she stood up quietly and walked a short distance away. There she brought the horses out of her bracelet. Chrissy stroked them and talked to them, trying to pass the time.

Soon, Lisa and Claudia woke up and came to Chrissy. They decided to try and make a fire for breakfast. The three gathered around the fire pit, leaving the horses by themselves off to the side. There was a small pile of kindling next to the pit, which they arranged in it. Chrissy wished she had remembered to bring matches, and hoped that Lisa had. Lisa, of course, did remember to bring matches, but she handed them to Claudia. "Chrissy and I will go collect firewood, and you can tend to the fire. Don't let the horses get too far away; we must stay as close together as possible in this unknown land." Chrissy dumped her backpack next to the fire pit and followed Lisa to collect wood.

Unfortunately, a pine forest is not the best place for firewood. All they could find were a few small branches and a *lot* of pine needles. "We could just bring lots and lots and lots of pine needles; they're easy to burn," Chrissy suggested.

"No," Lisa replied grimly. "Pine needles make a lot of smoke and not much heat. We don't want people knowing we're here." After foraging the forest floor for a few more minutes, she sighed. "We'll just have to use magic, then."

"Why couldn't we have done that first?" Chrissy asked.

"Because when the people of the village return, they'll sense that magic was used. They're not too fond of magic, either. Anyway, if they know there's magic around, they'll be able to trace it, and that's not very good. It would have been better to use normal firewood, but since there's none, we have to use magic."

The two girls turned around and started back to their campsite. As they were walking, Chrissy's stomach growled loudly. She started thinking of the wonderful food Russ and Alex would make while their parents weren't home. She stumbled over roots and rocks, lost in thought. Suddenly, a rope snagged Chrissy's ankle. It snaked through the grass and up the nearest tree, growing taut. Chrissy found herself being pulled off her feet and hoisted upside-down into the air.

Lisa started forward, and Chrissy shouted, "No, Lisa don't-" but another rope caught Lisa's foot, and soon both of them were hanging upside down like blankets on a clothesline.

The tips of Chrissy's hair brushed against the ground, and all her blood started rushing to her head. She was unable to see Lisa, but she could hear her muttering, "I was so stupid . . . why would they ever completely desert their village? How could I have led us into this mess?" Chrissy could say nothing.

Soon Chrissy saw feet marching toward them. Straining to look up, she could see a dozen people wearing long black cloaks. Faces unemotional, they approached the two girls, one synchronized step after another. Once they were about three feet away, the leading man stopped. The others separated and formed a circle around the girls. All this was done without a word.

After intently studying the two hanging people in front of him, the leader finally spoke. "Intruders, you are not welcome here." His voice was icy and cruel.

"You think they figured that out yet?" rasped another man across the circle. Some others laughed.

"Silence!" the leader barked. Turning back to the girls, he said, "Did you really think that you could trespass without our notice? Did you think that we would completely leave our village for you?" He paused to let laughter ring through the woods. "The question is, what should we do with you?"

Many unpleasant answers rang in Chrissy's ears. "Leave 'em out here to starve!"

"Let 'em be wolf-food!"

"Make 'em slaves!"

Chrissy shivered, and the rope swayed. Her foot was losing circulation, and her head felt like it was going to fall off. While threats still flew through the air, she faintly heard Lisa muttering something. Looking over, she saw the ropes around Lisa's foot slowly untying themselves, inch by inch.

They needed a distraction. If only they could get everyone's attention away from Lisa, she could untie herself and somehow get them out of there. Chrissy thought fast, but her thoughts were interrupted by the glorious sound of thundering hooves.

Claudia galloped into the clearing, astride Thunder. Alexis followed her foal, but Lightning was nowhere in sight. The circle of men broke as they all surged toward the sound. At the same time, the rope around Lisa's ankle whipped free. She flipped backward and landed nimbly on all fours, then raced to help Claudia, leaving Chrissy still hanging.

In the confusion, Claudia had been knocked sideways off Thunder's back, landing in the dirt. Two Quopes seized her, and three surged toward Lisa. The frightened horses trotted a short distance away. The plan had failed; they were still surrounded. Chrissy had almost given up hope when Lightning burst through the trees overhead. She spiraled toward the group of Quopes, dive-bombing them in a mass of flailing hooves and beating wings. The Quopes scattered.

Lisa pulled herself together and quickly summoned a protective wall between them and the Quopes. Alexis trotted over to where Chrissy was hanging. Chrissy clumsily clambered up until she was sitting cross-wise on Alexis's back, with one foot suspended in the air. Then she carefully leaned forward and untied the rope. The fact that Alexis was so tall greatly helped with this task.

Chrissy was about to jump off Alexis when Lisa requested, "Can you get the rope too please? It could come in handy." Chrissy agreed. She pulled the rope off the branch and handed it to Lisa, who stashed it in her satchel.

The next problem was how to get out of there. Lisa's walls encircled them, about twenty feet in diameter. Chrissy could see the Quopes gathering around them, waiting for them to try and leave. Lightning might help, but she wouldn't be able to carry all three of them out of the forest of Minakia. She might hold two, but Chrissy hated the idea of leaving someone behind.

Chrissy was stumped for a plan, but Lisa was not. "Put Alexis away," she told them. "Go on Lightning and fly to the edge of the forest. I'll meet you there."

"No, I won't leave without you!" Chrissy cried.

"Go!" Lisa ordered. "I've been through quick escapes before." Her tone had turned bitter, and Chrissy decided it was best to do as she was told.

Chrissy tucked Alexis safely into her charm bracelet and climbed onto Lightning's back. Claudia clambered on behind her.

When the Quopes saw what they were about to do, they started getting angry. They pounded on Lisa's protective walls, which flickered weakly. Chrissy nudged Lightning and they lifted into the air with a sweep of her great wings. Chrissy looked down and watched apprehensively to see what Lisa would do next.

Lisa mounted Thunder and reached for something in her satchel. Chrissy, moving farther and farther away, couldn't see what it was. Suddenly, Lisa's walls vanished and the Quopes surged forward. Lisa flung whatever it was in her hand on the ground and it immediately started emitting thick black smoke. Thunder's black coat blended in perfectly with the smoke, helping to shield them from the Quopes' eyes as they galloped off in the direction that Lightning was heading.

A tree passed in front, blocking the scene from Chrissy's view. She faced forward and studied the area in front of her. She could see the line of pines break at the edge of Minakia, but that was far in the distance. Lightning might not make it that long.

Claudia was squeezing Chrissy very tightly. "Are you okay?" Chrissy called to her over the sound of the rushing wind.

"Fine," she muttered weakly. She didn't sound very fine to Chrissy, so she had Lightning dip a little closer to the ground. Claudia lightened up a little bit after that, but still held on tightly.

After a long while, Chrissy could sense that Lightning was very tired. The edge of Minakia was close, so she decided to land and try walking the rest of the way. It wasn't very safe; someone might be around the edge looking for them, but it was safer than Lightning dropping out of the sky from exhaustion. Claudia seemed happier on the ground, too.

They walked for a few minutes. Suddenly, they heard the sound of galloping hooves right behind them. Chrissy froze in terror. The hoof beats approached, and she turned slowly to see who it was. A black horse and his rider were slowly coming into view . . . it was Lisa and Thunder! Chrissy ran to greet them and leaned on Thunder's broad, hot neck. "I'm glad we're all safe, but we must keep going," Lisa prompted. "This place is still dangerous."

The three hurried forward, and in a few minutes they were out of Minakia. The bright, lively trees and noisy chattering of birds greeted them like a "Welcome to Colorado!" sign would as you passed between states. Chrissy felt as relieved to see this as one would after driving for hours.

Chapter 18

*O*nce they were safe and out of Minakia, Chrissy's hunger flared up; they hadn't had any breakfast or a very big dinner. When she brought this up, Lisa stopped and sighed. "Yes, I'm hungry too. We can't do much on empty stomachs, so . . ." She emptied her satchel on a nearby tree-stump. They scarfed down their entire food supply, letting the horses graze on grass.

Now, hunger satisfied, the three thought about what to do next. "Well, we know for one thing; Luther isn't with the Quopes," Lisa said briskly.

"How do you know?" Chrissy asked.

"Because if he had, *he* would have been leading the group instead of the leader that was with them."

"What if he went to a different village?"

"He would still be the first to know that there were intruders in Minakia, and he would *definitely* be the first to respond."

After a long pause, Chrissy asked, "So where should we go now?"

"To the marketplace," Lisa decided. "There we should be able to get food, supplies, and news." She ticked each one off on her fingers. "News is important, just to hear if anything is going on that we should know about."

Chrissy let out Alexis and climbed onto her back. Once they were ready, the three girls set off to the marketplace. After a few silent minutes, Claudia asked a question. "Why can't you just find Luther with your necklace and his ring, like he did to find you?"

Lisa paused. "That would be a great idea, except that Luther's ring was destroyed with the connection stone when it broke. So, we just have to guess where he is."

"Oh." Claudia was disappointed that her idea wouldn't work. They plodded slowly onward, each lost in their own thoughts.

Once, Lightning suddenly stretched her wings and lifted off the ground. Claudia squealed and almost fell off. She tipped dangerously backward, and then clung tightly to Lightning's neck. The poor horse only wanted to stretch her wings. After a few minutes, they landed on the ground again, windblown.

A cluster of tarps, tents, and small buildings appeared through the endless maze of trees; they were nearing the marketplace. The travelers all started filling with anxiety. Thunder started getting skittish and jumpy. Lightning's wings fluttered half-heartedly. The riders shifted uncomfortably.

Only Alexis seemed to be slowing down instead of speeding up. Chrissy sensed her tiredness and felt bad about riding her all day. Suddenly Alexis stumbled. She pitched forward, and Chrissy tumbled over her neck into the dirt.

Alexis righted herself but stood with her right foreleg raised gingerly. Chrissy, however, stayed on the ground, aching all over. She heard two thuds, and Claudia and Lisa peered at her with concern in their faces. "I'm okay," she told them, and slowly pushed herself to her feet. She tested all her joints, deciding that nothing was broken or damaged.

Lisa squatted down next to Alexis and examined her hoof, holding it gently. There was something wedged deep in Alexis's hoof. Lisa wasn't an expert on hoof-care, and she didn't want to try to pull this out. They were lucky to be so close to the marketplace; there would definitely be a stable somewhere and we might be able to find a farrier too.

Claudia offered to walk to the marketplace, so Chrissy mounted Lightning, Lisa mounted Thunder, and Claudia led Alexis through the trees.

As they drew nearer and nearer to the tents, the three travelers started to hear music dancing toward them. People flooded in between the tents, talking and laughing. What caught Chrissy's attention most was the delicious aroma floating in the air. The horses sensed the excitement too, and they bobbed their heads and trotted a little faster.

If Chrissy had thought that one young girl leading an injured horse and two more riding bareback out of the forest would look suspicious, she had been *much* mistaken; the throngs of people surging around the marketplace didn't look twice at anything. They were focused on their errands, and nothing else. Chrissy was grateful for that, though; the less attention they got, the less likely it was that Luther would hear about them.

As the three horses squeezed through the crowd, it felt a lot like wading through a river, with people rushing past them. They found a horse-care tent and veered away from the main street to walk toward it.

At the entrance to the tent, a business-like man stood checking the customers coming in. His black hair hung in sheets around his face, but his steely gray eyes were set to catch anything suspicious.

Lisa slid off Thunder's back and reached into her satchel. She produced a couple of gold coins and gave them to the man. He handed Lisa three slips of paper, nodded curtly at the three of them, and they passed into the tent.

Inside, there were rows and rows of stalls. Horses greeted the girls from all sides. In the back of the tent, there was an open space where one man was brushing his horse. Lisa looked at the papers, and then studied the stall doors. "There! Thirteen, fourteen, and fifteen. Those are ours," she said pointing to three empty stalls. The faded yellow numbers that were painted on the doors marked the stalls that they had just rented.

They led their horses to the back, where each girl picked up a brush and groomed them. Alexis leaned up against Chrissy's brush, loving every moment. Chrissy, however, did not; after two days riding bareback in the forest, the horses were dirty!

After the horses' coats had been brushed to a shine and their manes had been combed completely smooth, the girls put Thunder and Lightning in their stalls and Lisa led Alexis toward the front of the tent. She asked the man at the front if they had a farrier business. He started grumbling to himself.

"Not usually . . . but under the circumstances . . ." He eyed Lisa's satchel, wondering how many more gold coins could be in it. Lisa reached in, grabbed some more coins, and poured them over the man's hand, allowing them to spill over the edge and onto the ground. He hefted the coins in his hands, considering for a moment.

"You got yourself a deal. Let your horse into that pen over on the right side of my tent, and I'll see who'll take the job." He dumped his coins into a leather pouch from his pocket, and hastily picked up the ones on the ground. "It'll take a while to find someone, so don't wait for me. I'll get your horse checked out and tell you the news when you come around." Chrissy didn't like that idea much, but Lisa pushed her along.

Chrissy, Claudia, Lisa, and Alexis headed over to the pen that the man had indicated, while the man walked away, looking around anxiously. "He looks a little suspicious, doesn't he?" Chrissy asked as Alexis looked around the corral.

"Everyone around the marketplace looks like that," Lisa explained. "He'll keep to his word; he's got plenty of business he wouldn't want to lose." Lisa's experience with the marketplace showed, and Chrissy decided not to argue.

They agreed to stop at the inn for lunch, since the man had said he'd be a while. As Chrissy stepped through the doorway, it took a few seconds to get her eyes adjusted to the dim light. Several people sat on stools in front of a long counter, talking loudly to each other and drinking from large mugs. Behind the counter stood a tired-looking man serving drinks and appetizers. Around the rest of the room were tables and chairs littered with napkins and cups. In the back was a staircase leading to the upper rooms.

Lisa led the way to an empty table. She sat down in one chair and Chrissy slid into the one opposite her. Claudia slumped into the last chair, next to Chrissy. They chatted idly, but everyone seemed restless. Suddenly Lisa stood up and went to get drinks. She came back with two steaming mugs of hot chocolate, for Chrissy and Claudia, and a mysterious bubbling green liquid for herself.

Chrissy took one sip and sighed; it was delicious. It filled her up with new energy, helping her to plan their next move. "So, after this, we're going to stock up on food and check on Alexis. Then we should be on our way . . . where?"

The girls tried to think of places Luther might hide, but no place they thought of seemed likely. A waitress came by and offered them sandwiches from a tray. They each took one and munched quietly, ideas failing them. With nothing coming to mind, Claudia suggested that they check on Alexis, so they filed out into the sunshine.

When they got back to the corral, Alexis was still wandering around, bored. It looked like nothing had happened yet. Chrissy went into the tent and took an apple from the basket. She came back out again and gave the apple to Alexis, who whinnied thankfully.

Lisa and Chrissy went to replenish their food supply, while Claudia stayed behind with Alexis. She messed around absentmindedly while she waited. *How long does it take to find a farrier?* Claudia wondered. She leaned against the fence and watched for anyone coming.

Out of the haze, Claudia saw the man from the tent coming toward her, followed by a new girl. She had wild red hair and her clothes were splattered with mud. She carried a brown leather bag of tools, and looked completely out of place next to the grim-faced, no-nonsense man she was walking with.

Claudia nearly laughed at the sight of them, but she was afraid of being alone with them while they checked Alexis.

She was therefore relieved at the sight of Chrissy and Lisa walking nearer from the other direction, bags bulging.

The two pairs met at the corral and entered together. "Kerry Latice," the woman introduced herself, shaking Chrissy's hand.

"I'm Chrissy," Chrissy tried to smile, but ended up with a grimace; the girl's grip was very strong and Chrissy's hand was throbbing. Kerry went around to each girl and introduced herself, shaking hands.

The man cleared his throat loudly. "Ms Latice is the best horse-person around here, and I trust her to do her stuff. So, if you'll excuse me, I'd like to get back to work." The girls thanked him and, as he left with his back turned to them, Claudia thought, *Good riddance!*

Kerry took out a string and tied her hair back. A few wisps straggled out, but she brushed them aside. She set down her bag and approached Alexis. "And this is Alexis," she sighed. "You pretty girl, do you have something stuck in your foot?" Kerry reached out to Alexis and stroked her mane and down her back. "The right foreleg?" she asked.

"Yes," Chrissy replied. Kerry quietly took her bag and set it down next to the horse. Then she gently raised Alexis's right foreleg to look at the hoof. "Oh my!" she gasped.

After a thorough inspection, Kerry confirmed that there was a piece of rock lodged deep in Alexis's hoof. Walking on it would push it in deeper. She could try to take it out, or let it heal on its own. The healing would take weeks if she stayed off the leg, but trying to pull it out would be challenging because it was so deep. Chrissy thought for a while. Then she decided that Kerry should try to take it out.

Kerry worked silently. Alexis fidgeted occasionally, but was otherwise very good. She stood as still as possible while Kerry carefully pulled the rock out of her hoof. At last, Kerry got it out. "There's the little rascal!" she cried triumphantly.

It was a large shard of black rock, sharp on the edges. There was a tiny bead of blood on the tip, glistening in the sun, and Chrissy shuddered, realizing what it was. Lisa held out her hand to Kerry, who dropped the rock into it. Then Lisa said in a strained voice, "Thank you so much Kerry. You've been a big help, but we've gotta go soon."

"Sure!" Kerry got the gist that she wasn't really wanted, so she gathered her things and exited the pen. As she walked away, she called behind her shoulder, "You shouldn't ride her for a bit; just to give it time to heal, but it'll be okay after a few days."

"Thanks!" Chrissy waited until Kerry was out of sight, and then turned to look at Lisa.

Lisa was staring at the chip of rock like it was part of another planet. "Obsidian," she muttered. Chrissy could almost see the thoughts churning in her mind, but didn't interrupt them.

Everything was silent, except for the distant bustling of the marketplace and Alexis scuffling around the pen. Finally, Claudia voiced what they were all thinking. "The connection stone." It was only a shard, but it was unmistakable, this tiny bit of rock was obsidian, part of the connection stone Luther had used not even two weeks ago. When Alexis cracked it, it shattered into many pieces. Lisa had sent each piece to a different protected magical place so that Luther couldn't find them, so how did it get in Alexis's hoof?

"You said the pieces were in magical places-"

"I didn't see exactly where, just the magical content in each place," Lisa replied quickly.

"Was there something particularly magical in the forest that she might have stepped on?" Claudia asked.

"I'm not sure." Lisa continued studying the rock. "It has her blood on it," she said suddenly.

"Is that bad?" Chrissy asked.

"Could be good, could be bad."

Suddenly Lisa's head snapped up. She looked around suspiciously. Tucking the obsidian in her satchel, she said, "Let's go."

* * *

They were plodding along on an old dirt road. Lisa rode Thunder, Claudia rode Lightning, and Chrissy walked, having put Alexis away in her bracelet to rest. The road paralleled the woods, which was on their right. To their left lay a great expanse of hay and corn fields. The landscape stayed the same for hours, on and on as far as the eye could see. Every once and a while the girls would switch off who was walking and who was riding. Chrissy didn't know where they were going, she just followed Lisa. They passed no one.

The girls faced the sun, which was slowly setting on the horizon. The wind started tugging at them. Chrissy felt exhausted from the long day. She suggested that they try to have dinner and find somewhere to sleep. The rest agreed, so Lisa turned into the forest. They walked a short distance in, just out of sight of the road, in case someone came by in the night. Chrissy put the horses safely into her bracelet and wondered what they could have for dinner.

Claudia suggested they take a few cobs of corn from the fields. "That would be stealing," Chrissy pointed out. "But we could make a fire and toast some bread."

"That sounds good," Lisa said. "You two make the fire and I'll get our shelter ready. Chrissy, can I see your backpack?" Chrissy took it off and handed it to Lisa, who dug around and came up with a knife and the rope. She cut the rope in half, and then climbed up the nearest tree.

"Lisa, do you know what you're doing?" Chrissy asked her.

"Of course! Just keep making the fire. There are matches in my bag."

"Fine," Chrissy muttered, going to collect wood for Claudia to make a fire. Thankfully, this forest had more brushwood than the forest of Minakia, and Chrissy found a good-sized pile in no time.

When Chrissy returned to their campsite, she saw that Claudia had brushed away most of the dirt and leaves in one spot and made a ring of rocks inside it. Then she collected some kindling out of the twigs around her, and lit a match. Chrissy was just dumping her pile a few feet away when the match caught and a tiny flame appeared.

"Yes!" Claudia cried. "I did it!" She added a few more sticks and the fire was soon blazing.

Then Chrissy remembered that Lisa had been working on the shelter. She looked over to where Lisa had climbed up a tree. There were two parallel ropes tied securely to the branches of four trees. Chrissy watched as Lisa flung a blanket from Claudia's bag over top of the ropes, and then hurried over to help. Together, they draped two more blankets over each side of the ropes to form the walls.

Chrissy ducked under the blanket and peered around her temporary bedroom. It wasn't much, but it would protect them a little in case it rained, and it blocked the awful wind that was starting up. It seemed pretty roomy, and not much of a squeeze. Chrissy rather liked it.

"The fire's ready for toastin'," Claudia called. Chrissy ducked out of their makeshift room and walked toward the fire.

Claudia had stoked up the fire and there were embers sizzling on the bottom. Chrissy sifted through Lisa's satchel and produced a loaf of bread. Then she found a long, thin, almost straight stick and stuck the bread on it like a bread-kabob. Then she put the stick over the fire. Every few moments, Chrissy turned the stick, until the bread was golden brown all around.

When it was done, Chrissy pulled the bread off the stick and ducked into the "bedroom." She found that Claudia and Lisa had cleared away all the sticks and leaves on the ground. She sat down and tore the loaf into three pieces. Chrissy took one piece and gave the others to her friends. They munched in silence, or as silently as one could munch on toasted bread. Once they were finished with the bread, Lisa brought out some fruit.

After discussing their plans and other ideas, the three girls arranged themselves to lie down for sleep. Chrissy used her backpack as a pillow. They tried to fall asleep, listening to the chorus of crickets and the blankets swaying softly.

*   *   *

Heat hung like a blanket over the area. Chrissy was running, running for all she was worth. She tried to get away from someone, but an invisible force pushed Chrissy off her feet. She was suspended above a fiery expanse, with nothing to keep her from falling. As she looked down, the bright red lava dimmed. It slowly stopped dancing, and faded to a dull red color. It was strangely the same color of a blanket floating in the back of her mind . . .

*   *   *

Chrissy gradually became aware that she was awake. The blanket above her came into focus, and she started to notice birds chirping somewhere. She sat up, body aching. Chrissy saw that Lisa was already up, but Claudia was just now waking with Chrissy. They stood up together, rubbing their eyes, and left their shelter.

Outside, Lisa was stirring the dead coals from last night's fire. In a few minutes, a small flame flared back up. After adding more twigs and sticks, it roared to life. They warmed themselves while enjoying their breakfast together.

Chrissy let the horses out, gave them apples, and let them graze a bit. Then she checked Alexis's hoof. It was cracked down the center. The edges of the crack were blackened. Chrissy alerted Lisa at once.

Bending over to examine the hoof, Lisa said, "That's bad. It has to be from the obsidian. There was blood on it, which means it got in her bloodstream. No farrier would know what this is, but I do, there's evil magic in Alexis's veins. And the only way to cure magic is with more magic. We have to go to Lasceri."

"What's Lasceri?" Chrissy asked.

"It's where your rock came from. Lasceri is a cliff overlooking the Poget Sea, and it's also the strongest source of magic I know of around here. The only way to cure this obsidian poison is to go to Lasceri and use the magic inside the rocks to destroy it. This will set us back in our search for Luther, but Alexis is in a serious predicament, we have no time to spare."

"If my rock is from Lasceri, then why can't we use this?" Chrissy lifted her necklace.

"It's not powerful enough." Lisa set down Alexis's hoof and started putting out the fire. "Put Alexis away to rest and let's pack up. The sooner we leave, the sooner we get there, and the sooner we get there, the better." She pulled down the blankets, and Chrissy and Claudia helped her take down the ropes and put the blankets away.

Once they were packed up and ready to go, the girls set off down the old road, this time with renewed vigor. They crossed through fields and meadows, following Lisa, who was rubbing her necklace and muttering to herself as if it were telling her directions. They stopped for a drink at a water pump on the outskirts of a farm, and kept going. The sun was high in the sky, and Chrissy guessed it was about noon.

Finally, the endless fields gave way to dirt mixed with rocks. As they continued, the dirt dwindled until they were walking on plain grey rocks. If this was the all-magical Lasceri Lisa was talking about, then Chrissy couldn't tell *magical* rocks from any plain old rock. Soon she realized this wasn't the Lasceri that Lisa was talking about. Lisa looked suspiciously at the few people dotted about, then told Chrissy to put Thunder and Lightning away as she crept forward. Chrissy did as she was told and followed after her.

Up until now, the surface of rock had been relatively flat, but now it sloped steeply upward and reached the sky. A red sign stood at the foot of this hill and stated clearly:

Caution:
Unsafe Slope
Do Not Climb

Lisa walked up to the sign. She made sure no one was looking, then waved her hand at it. The sign wavered, then dissolved, revealing a dark tunnel leading directly into the face of the rock. She walked straight into it. Claudia nervously followed her, and Chrissy brought up the rear.

The tunnel sealed itself behind them, and Chrissy shivered. Darkness closed around the girls, but Lisa walked on. Chrissy held her hands out to keep from bumping into anything. She tried to keep them in front of her, instead of touching the slimy, mossy walls of the tunnel. Soon, a pinprick of light outlined someone's head in front of her. They continued toward the light, which grew brighter as they went along, and finally Chrissy stepped out of the tunnel.

Chrissy blinked as she found herself in broad sunlight. White rocks stretched out before her, and she could hear gulls and the sound of the sea not far off. That had to be the Poget Sea Lisa spoke of. In front of her, there was a circular hill of rocks with a cratered center, like a smushed donut. Lisa headed straight for the donut.

Chrissy let Alexis out. At first, she took in her surroundings, then started shifting nervously from hoof to hoof. Chrissy led her after Lisa.

They crested the small hill and started down the dip. Lisa crouched down and examined the rock in the center of the circle. Chrissy bent over and felt it too. It was surprisingly warm. After a few seconds, she noticed that the rock seemed to be pulsing. Yes, there was definitely a rhythm to the slight waves on the surface of the rock.

"Is this pulse the magic in the rock?" Claudia asked from behind Chrissy.

"Yes. There's so much magic in this rock formation that it travels out in pulses, like a radio. That's why it will heal Alexis; we just need to direct one of the waves into her hoof and it will destroy the poison from the obsidian." She listened intently for a few seconds, and then slapped her hand down on the rock.

Golden sparks shot from where Lisa's hand touched, and the rock glowed beneath her hand. Chrissy could actually see the power wave this time, golden and rippling out from the center of the rock like the ripples a drip makes in a lake.

In a second, it stopped. Suddenly, the ground trembled. Lisa lost her balance and started tumbling toward the center of the rock. As she neared the center, a hole opened in the rock. Chrissy reached out to grab Lisa's hand as Lisa scrambled to get a hold on anything, but they weren't quick enough; Lisa tumbled into blackness!

"Lisa!" Chrissy cried. "Alexis, stay. Claudia, come on, we have to save her!" Chrissy grabbed Claudia's hand and together, the two friends leaped into the gaping black hole, falling down into darkness.

Chapter 19

She was falling, falling. Wind whistled past her ears and through her hair. Chrissy looked down and saw lava, growing closer and closer, threatening to envelope her. Then she noticed a slab of rock on the surface of the lava that they seemed to be heading toward.

Chrissy saw Lisa standing weakly on the rock. Lisa raised her hand and pointed it at them. At once Chrissy felt herself slow down. She braced her legs and pointed them at the ground. As she reached the rock, her knees buckled and she crouched on all fours, panting. Hearing Claudia hit the ground too, Chrissy tried to sit up.

This rock was grey-black, quite different from the white above. They were surrounded by lava on three sides, but to Chrissy's right the rock led to four different tunnels in the side of a solid rock wall.

Chrissy stood up unsteadily. "Did you know about that portal?" she asked Lisa.

"No," Lisa replied, eyes wide, taking everything in. "But someone must." She pointed to a lighted torch inside one of the tunnels. Chrissy glanced at it and agreed. In fact, the torch looked like it was bobbing toward them! It was, along with the sound of many pounding feet. Soon, figures focused in Chrissy's view.

At the front of the procession, carrying the torch, was Luther Rehtul. His face was pale. His clothes were tattered. Luther led a throng of people marching through the tunnel. Chrissy couldn't see much facial expression in the flickering of the torch, but he didn't seem to have the smugness he usually had, and Chrissy had seen that smugness in him *a lot*. Luther reached the end of the tunnel and set the torch into an empty metal bracket by the entrance.

"Welcome, girls," Luther sneered, almost as if he had expected them. Chrissy, Lisa, and Claudia didn't try to run. It wouldn't have done any good anyway, for seconds later more troops filled every tunnel. "Let's go," Luther ordered.

The three girls just let themselves be led away through Luther's tunnel. Chrissy was extremely scared, but it gave her satisfaction to see Luther acting so awkwardly; he had expected a fight, and it was embarrassing for him to bring so many troops when the girls just walked away like they were meeting someone at the park.

Lisa didn't waste her energy fighting, she just studied everything around her. She looked at each person marching around them, and their weapons. She looked at the rock walls of the cave around them. She studied where they were going in the tunnel up ahead. Finally, Luther snapped, "Stop looking around so much, you nosy girl!" After that, Lisa concentrated on one thing just out of her vision. Chrissy expected something to explode, the way Lisa's eyes glazed, and Chrissy could practically hear her mind buzzing, but nothing happened.

Chrissy controlled her fear right up until she found out they were going to be imprisoned separately. "What?" she squeaked.

"Oh, yes," Luther's eyes glinted this time. "You each get your own room!"

*   *   *

Chrissy had stayed in much better rooms before. The rock was cold and hard. She had nothing to sit on except the floor. The only light was that seeping through the bars on the tiny window of her metal door. They had taken her backpack and necklace, Lisa's bag and necklace, Claudia's bag, and the obsidian piece, before slamming the door shut with a clang and marching away through the winding tunnels.

Chrissy tried to peer through her window, but could only see the wall across from her cell. She tried to stick her arm through the bars, but they were too close together. She didn't really think the cell was sealed with a normal lock; Luther wouldn't be that foolish and simple. He would definitely have some sort of spell on it. There didn't seem to be another way to get out other than the door. That was the good thing about having a cell in rock, or—in Chrissy's case—the bad thing.

Sliding down the wall, Chrissy sat down in despair. She rubbed her hand against the wall behind her, remembering how she had done just the same to the tree in her backyard with her rock, except this time it didn't uncover a new world or get her out of her predicament.

Commotion outside the door startled Chrissy. She realized she must have somehow dozed off. She jumped up and stared through the window with difficulty.

Chrissy must be hallucinating. Really. There was no way that little wood figurine could have come all this way. But there was Chrissy Jr., stumbling through the tunnel and looking around. "Chrissy!" Chrissy whispered to her. Chrissy Jr. started, and rushed to the cell door. "How did you get here?"

Chrissy Jr. smiled. "I know when you're in trouble. I got here as fast as I could, but these tunnels are a nightmare."

"Do you know how to open this?"

"Oh, simple!" Chrissy Jr. thrust her hand at the door handle that Chrissy couldn't see. Her hand glowed purple, sparks shot toward the door, and it swung open.

Chrissy stepped out. "Wow."

Chrissy Jr. shrugged. "It's the leximer in me; it can fix anything."

"Cool. And thanks," Chrissy hugged her. "Now, let's go find Claudia."

It took a while for the two girls to find Claudia's cell through the winding passages, but they finally found her. Chrissy Jr. did her special hand trick while Chrissy explained, and Claudia was freed too. Chrissy Jr. staggered a bit and leaned against the wall, eyes closed. "Are you okay?" Claudia asked.

"Apparently not," Chrissy reasoned. "It's like giving blood, and this is the second time she's done it in twenty minutes. We can't do this again for Lisa, but I had some leximer in my backpack. If only I still had my backpack, we could use it."

"Then let's see where they put your backpack," Chrissy Jr. said weakly. She leaned on Chrissy's shoulder and they struggled through the passages.

Soon Chrissy heard noises other than their scuffling feet. Peering around the corner, she saw a room in the side of the corridor to their left. A person was sitting in a chair with his back turned to the door. He was playing with Chrissy's flashlight, turning it on and shining it on the wall, then flicking the switch off. He seemed intrigued by it, and Chrissy hoped his interest would keep him occupied for just a few seconds more.

Chrissy snuck around the corner and quietly entered the room. A table stood between her and the man, with the contents of her backpack spilled all over it. Chrissy carefully picked up her necklace and put it around her neck. Then she tried to pick up the leather pouch of leximer, which she didn't realize was partly under her hairbrush. When she lifted the pouch, her brush clinked against the rock table.

The man whirled around and grabbed Chrissy's arm. His eyes grew wide and he used the other hand to snatch the pouch back. Chrissy tried to jerk her hand away, but the pouch ripped and leximer spilled everywhere.

Some landed on the man's hand, and he let go, staring at it. Some landed on Chrissy's arm, and it tingled sensationally. She quickly cradled the pieces of leather to hold whatever liquid hadn't spilled. Running to Chrissy Jr., she poured it into her hand. The leximer seemed to soak into her skin, and Chrissy Jr. took a deep breath. She looked strengthened, filled with new energy.

Meanwhile, the man in the room had been staring at his hand, which was smoking. Suddenly, he jerked awake, as if from a trance, and blinked around. Then, as if seeing Chrissy for the first time, he hugged her!

Looking over the man's shoulder, Chrissy raised her eyebrows at Claudia, who shrugged. When the man let go, he explained, "I'm Liam, one of the guardians of Lasceri. We have lived peacefully here until Luther came. He enchanted us to do his will, and forget who we really were. But it must have been the leximer's magic that freed me from the curse, so I thank you."

"You're welcome," Chrissy said awkwardly. "Listen, my name is Chrissy, and this is Claudia. We're here to help you get rid of Luther."

"Great!"

Chrissy thought for just a second. "Do you know where we could get extra leximer?"

"We have a whole supply for emergencies, and I know where it is. We can also retrieve your things."

"Okay, so you and Claudia go get as much as you can. Revive as many guardians as you can, but *find Lisa*. She'll know what to do. As for Chrissy Jr. and I, we'll find Luther. Let's go."

The two pairs set off through the tunnels on their different ways. Chrissy and Chrissy randomly picked corridors whenever they came to a fork, and eventually found themselves back out in the open lava lake Chrissy had fallen near. She thought she saw a figure standing across the flat rock through the heat waves, and she walked toward it.

The figure was a few yards away, but Chrissy couldn't seem to get near it. She was definitely moving forward, but the figure wasn't coming closer. Finally, the image disappeared, and the two girls were at the edge of the great lava expanse. She could see nothing out there. Suddenly, Chrissy Jr. cried, "No, this isn't right, go back-" she whirled around, but a voice cracked through hers like ice.

"Well, well, well. This is the amazing girl who ruined my plans, with a twin? You two are in a great position to trick people, but here you are, taking advantage of nothing. I thought you outsmarted Luther, but now I understand that you are all just stupid." A pale, wispy man looking remarkably like Luther stood a few feet away, between the girls and the tunnels. He moved slowly toward them, looking amused. Chrissy knew she remembered him from somewhere, and then she realized this was Luther's father, the man in her dream. He seemed more solid now, stronger than he was in her dream. She tried to stall and give herself time to think, but a distraction came almost instantly.

Claudia appeared out of the far right tunnel. She was followed by Liam and seven other guardians. They were coming at Luther's father. Chrissy and Chrissy Jr. darted sideways in opposite directions, away from the man and out of the way of the people charging him. The man somehow knew he was being attacked from behind, and he turned around before the guardians even got close to him.

With a wave of his hand the man stopped the attackers in their tracks. They stood there, struggling against invisible bonds. In the same instant, Chrissy was slammed against the wall behind her and pinned there. Without a wall at her back, Chrissy Jr. was swept off her feet and suspended in the air. Her eyes widened huge and her feet flailed hopelessly. The man cackled. Again, Chrissy remembered this scene;

she saw it in the dream she had in the tent, except that it was Chrissy Jr. floating in the air, not her.

"You see, I cannot be surprised or overtaken. My only downfall last time was lack of power, but I have that fixed now. I'm taking Luther's power," he explained smugly. That's why he looked stronger, Chrissy thought. "Combining it with my own power makes me stronger and I will soon be restored to my true state," he continued. "It is happening right now. The process is almost complete, and no one can stop me!"

"I wouldn't count on it!" echoed two voices from the direction of the tunnels. Lisa and Luther stood side by side, facing their father.

Chapter 20

*A*s the man whipped around to focus on his children, his enchantments broke. Chrissy Jr. plummeted toward the lava, screaming. With a sweep of her hand, Lisa eased her safely back to the ground. Chrissy fell onto her hands and got back up, shaking. Claudia and the guardians unfroze and backed out of the menacing glares between the father and kids.

"Lisa," the man snarled. "You always meddled into things you didn't understand. And Luther, how dare you?" Immediately, hundreds of other guardians surged out of the tunnel entrances, far outnumbering the eight freed ones. Lisa and Luther stepped forward, surrounded. When their father roared, the fight broke out.

Flashes of light exploded from all directions. Chrissy ducked under a stream of sparks shooting from who knows where. A guardian stepped through the smoke and grabbed her. She kicked and squirmed, but his grip was too strong.

Suddenly Lisa appeared and blasted him off his feet. "Chrissy!" she yelled over the commotion. "Get to Liam. Tell him it's time to put the pieces back; he'll know what to do." Then she ran off.

Chrissy darted through the crowd. Spotting Claudia, she grabbed her hand and kept running. They approached

Liam, who was helping Chrissy Jr. to revive all the guardians. They passed Luther. "Putting the pieces back, are we?" he growled. "You'll need this." He pushed a white rock into Chrissy's hand. It was the exact same size as her rock. Luther disappeared before she could say anything.

Chrissy shouted to Liam, "Lisa says it's time to put the pieces back."

He knew what that meant. "For that we need to get back to the surface, but how?" Claudia dug around in her backpack and produced Chase, her little owl carving.

"He's not strong enough!" Chrissy cried.

"Yes he is!" Claudia insisted. She threw the statue into the air and called, "Chase!" The owl burst to life and flapped his grey wings, soaring over the battle. Then he dove toward the girls, hovering a few feet off the ground.

Liam disappeared into the crowd, and returned, followed by nine of the other guardians and Chrissy Jr. When they were ready to go, Claudia gripped Chase's tail. He soared up a few more feet until Claudia was dangling just above their heads. Chrissy reluctantly grabbed onto Claudia's ankle, and was suddenly filled with a bubbling sensation from head to toe. She felt light and airy, being lifted up for the others to grab on. The rest did the same until they formed a great line hanging in the air.

Chase flapped his wings hard, but he otherwise seemed undisturbed by all the extra weight hanging off him. As he rose higher and higher into the air above the battlefield, Chrissy watched Lisa and Luther, fighting back to back, fade into tiny specks. The cave ceiling was so high, it was black. They were soaring up into nothingness.

*   *   *

Landing back on the surface, a cool wind blew by. Chrissy felt refreshed, away from the steamy and humid underground cave. But her contentment didn't last long, they had a job to do and she had no idea what it was.

Hurrying over to Liam, Chrissy asked him what 'putting the pieces back' meant. "It means returning all the pieces of rock taken over the years and putting them back where they belong, on Lasceri," he explained. "All the guardians took a single piece to keep. Now we have to give them back."

"What will it do?" Chrissy asked.

"I don't know, but apparently Lisa thinks it will help."

"How do we give them back?"

"Just drop it."

Chrissy took the piece Luther gave her and dropped it onto the ground. It glowed purple and skittered a few feet to the left to latch itself in place on the rest of the rock.

All around the donut, guardians were dropping rocks onto the ground, which latched in place together. Once everyone had put their piece down, Chrissy held her breath. Nothing happened. Something was wrong, she knew it.

Suddenly, Chrissy remembered Lisa had said that her rock was from Lasceri! There was one piece missing; hers. She took off her necklace. With fumbling fingers, Chrissy took off the wire that wrapped around the rock. Finally, the last piece of Lasceri dropped with a clink.

Wind gusted along the flat ground. The waves in Poget Sea churned against the edge of the cliff. Then, one huge wave far off at sea started growing. It rose taller and taller, blocking out the sun. As it approached, they could see it rising above the top of the cliff, shimmering and turning purple. Chase flew straight toward the tunnel at the entrance of Lasceri, and the group followed, rushing to safety from the wave of leximer's reach.

The great wave crashed onto the cliff, surging everywhere and spraying them some. Foam frothed and swirled around, obscuring the donut from view. When it finally drained away back into the sea, the entire donut of Lasceri was gone.

Chunks of rock and boulders littered the edge of the cliff. The leximer had dissolved the cave somehow. Gripped by fear and worry, Chrissy couldn't bear to look into the sea. "Lisa," she whispered. Suddenly, she cried out, "Where's Alexis?" She had left the horse out here when Lisa had fallen down the portal, but they hadn't seen her when they were putting the pieces back, so where was she?

They spread out over the rock and searched for Alexis, but saw no sign of her. Suddenly, Chrissy heard a whinny ring through the air, coming from the sea. She scrambled down a few rocks of the cliff, and filled with relief; there was Alexis, picking her way up the cliff with Lisa on her back and Luther leading.

"Oh, yay, yay, yay!" Chrissy cried. She yelled happily to everyone else, "Guys, come here!" The guardians, Claudia, and Chrissy Jr. all gathered at the edge of the cliff and helped the three up. "Lisa!" Chrissy shouted for joy and Alexis stamped her hoof. "How's her hoof?"

"After walking in the leximer surf, I think she's fine," Lisa replied.

Luther walked a good distance away and stared into the horizon. "He's a little sensitive right now," Lisa explained.

"We should get back to the Winglet village, and then we'll have a great explaining party!"

When they were saying good-bye to the guardians, Liam asked if Chrissy Jr. could stay with the guardians on their travels. Chrissy Jr. seemed excited at that thought, and Chrissy wanted her to be happy. So they bid farewell to Chrissy Jr. too, and Chrissy, Claudia, Lisa, and Luther departed for the Winglet village.

Chapter 21

*T*hat group of cabins had never looked so welcoming. Chrissy was exhausted from the day's traveling, and the thought of finally sitting down on the couch with a cup of hot chocolate was so inviting.

After leaving Lasceri, Lisa, Luther, Chrissy, and Claudia had rested at a home on the coast of Poget Sea. The next morning they set off early and journeyed all day to get to the Winglet's village at dusk.

Now Matthew hurried out and welcomed them graciously, even Luther. They let the horses rest while they were bustled into a cabin. Chrissy and Claudia were wrapped in blankets and given hot chocolate. Chrissy sipped it quietly while the grown-ups rushed around talking with each other.

Finally, Lisa, Luther, Matthew, and several other adults sat down in the living room with Chrissy and Claudia. Chrissy set down her mug on the table and leaned forward to talk, but Lisa was the one who began their discussion.

"When Luther and I were young, we lived in the cave of Lasceri. The guardians of Lasceri were my parents' servants, but really my friends. They had ten special leaders who each had taken one rock from the surface, and Luther and I thought that sounded cool, so we both took one too.

When I came to your world, I lost mine by the tree, not knowing that it would become a key for someone else to get through. When you visited the Winglets for the first time, I felt the magic. Then I followed you to the library, and I saw your necklace. That confirmed that you had the rock I had lost. I knew we would have to meet again, and we did! You pretty much know the rest from there, so, Luther's turn!"

Luther cleared his throat and said gruffly, "Well, you know the beginning. Before Father sent me off, though, he put terrible thoughts in my mind. I was thinking about them for years. Later, Father started coming to me as a ghost. He told me to do things I would have never dreamed of on my own. He said I'd get more power by doing them." His eyes were downcast, and Luther stared at the floor in shame as he talked.

"Father could only stay in his ghostly form if he had enough power to keep him there. I thought the connection stone would give *me* more power, but he really intended its power for himself. Then, when I failed," here he grimaced, "Father decided to take a more direct route, taking *my* power."

Chrissy shivered, trying not to imagine it.

"Then, we were both back home in Lasceri, and Lisa saved me, after all I'd done . . ." he trailed off into silence.

"And now we're all fine and happy!" Matthew concluded brightly. "You four have had *quite* a day, so I suggest we all get some sleep, and figure out more tomorrow. Sound good?"

Chrissy thought that sounded lovely, and they all started filing out. Claudia invited Chrissy to stay at her cabin. As they said good-night to the others and headed to Claudia's cabin, Lisa led Luther off to her cabin, and Matthew made his way to his.

Claudia's parents welcomed the girls, and Chrissy collapsed onto a couch. She fell asleep almost as soon as her eyes closed.

*   *   *

Chrissy woke up very late, with sun streaming through the windows. Both girls were very hungry for breakfast and they sat with Claudia's family at the table. It was nice to finally have a full, hot, on-the-plate meal for the first time in days. Once breakfast was finished, the girls went up to the tree-house. Lisa, Luther, and Matthew were already there, discussing things. Lisa looked up and said cheerily, "Good morning!"

"Hey Lisa!" Chrissy replied.

Matthew was a bit more serious. "Hello, Chrissy. We were just talking about the events of your trip. You set things right for all of us, and things have been so much better for us since you first arrived. But . . ."

"But what?"

"We think, after putting your key back in Lasceri, that . . . you might not . . . be able to come back here once you leave."

Chrissy was shocked. "But-"

"We don't know how it works or why you could get here in the first place, but you won't be able to get back without the key. I'm so sorry."

Chrissy sank into a chair. "I . . ."

"Knowing that this will be hard, Lisa and I came up with a way for you two to keep in touch." Matthew produced two leather-bound books and handed one to Chrissy and one to Claudia. "When one of you writes in it, the writing will appear in the other journal." He handed Claudia a pen, who wrote on the first blank page: Hello, this is Claudia. Instantly, the exact words shone on Chrissy's book too.

"Wow! That's great! Thanks guys." Chrissy threw her arms around Lisa, who smiled.

"Let's go outside," Matthew suggested.

Out in the sun, Chrissy slowly walked over to the three horses. Hugging Alexis's neck, Chrissy told Claudia, "I want you to keep Thunder, Alexis, and Lightning."

"What?" Claudia gasped. "But they're yours!"

"They won't be able to play if I keep them. They'll have to be in my bracelet all the time. And I *know* you'll take care of them."

It took a minute to let it all sink in. "I will," she promised. Chrissy hugged her best friend.

The whole village gathered to say good-bye. Chrissy thanked each one of them. She hugged Lisa and Claudia, and shook Luther's hand.

Chrissy stepped up to the tree. Matthew stood next to her. "Good-bye, Chrissy." She took a deep breath, and stepped through to her world.

Epilogue

Chrissy raced off the bus and into her house. She hurriedly took off her shoes and ran upstairs. Dumping her backpack on the floor of her room, she sat down at her desk and opened her journal. There was a picture, hand drawn by Claudia. Chase was flying between the trees with Lightning close on the chase.

Acknowledgements

Special thanks to Samantha Neuman, Monica Bickerton, and Kristen Chrobak for long hours of editing support; W. Little for the wonderful horse illustration; Mark Neuman for image creation; and all my friends and family for their constant support and encouragement.

CPSIA information can be obtained at www.ICGtesting.com
Printed in the USA
BVOW07s1242280115

385378BV00001B/1/P